EVERNIGHT PUBLISHING ®

www.evernightpublishing.com

SAM CRESCENT

Copyright© 2014 Sam Crescent

ISBN: 978-0-3695-0638-2

Cover Artist: Sour Cherry Designs

Jacket Design: Jay Aheer

Editor: Karyn White

BLAINE: CHRISTMAS AT THE SKULLS

DEDICATION

I just want to wish everyone a very Merry Christmas.

BLAINE: CHRISTMAS AT THE SKULLS

BLAINE:
CHRISTMAS AT THE SKULLS

The Skulls, 10

Sam Crescent

Copyright © 2014

Prologue

"Blaine, what are you doing?" Emily asked, wringing her hands. Her stomach was in knots as she looked at the man who'd knocked her up. He was drinking hard yet again, and it looked like he was also high. Everything she'd heard about The Skulls had to be a complete lie. She'd thought they were a hard biker club but also a fair one. They didn't do drugs or allow drugs, yet Blaine's behavior as a prospect was getting more and more out of control.

"What does it look like I'm doing, woman? I'm having a good time. Maybe you should do it sometime." Blaine's eyes were bloodshot as he glared at her. This wasn't the man she'd come to know. There was no way she'd let this man anywhere near her. She tucked some hair behind her ear, feeling nervous.

She was pregnant, and any good time she could have was long gone. The only kind of fun she'd be experiencing in the future was changing diapers and feeding. The condom he'd used to take her virginity had broken leaving them both with this mess to deal with. She was eighteen years old and going to be a mother by the time she was nineteen. The prospect terrified her.

What terrified her more was the fact she knew, deep down in her gut, that she was about to do this all on her own. Blaine wasn't going to be there for her. She'd lost him the moment he decided to become a Skull, or maybe it was before that. Maybe he really didn't want to be a father. She didn't know the truth. Blaine was not the man she'd fallen in love with. This was someone else, someone vile and ugly to the core.

"For fuck's sake, Emily. If you're not going to party, fuck off. There are more than enough women here to party with."

Tears filled her eyes. She knew he hadn't been faithful to her. From the moment she'd met him, Blaine was the only person she could think about. He didn't feel the same way about her. She saw it now. Before he became part of the club, he'd been a different person. He was older than she was, in his early twenties, but she'd truly thought he was different. No, he had been different, but the man she'd come to know had changed. She didn't like the man he'd turned into.

One of the women, a club whore she'd heard them call her, wrapped her arms around Blaine's neck. "Hey, baby, she giving you a bad time?"

Feeling completely out of place, Emily took a step back then another. With each step back she took, she knew it was over. Blaine was never going to be in her life. She couldn't trust him, nor could she trust him with her unborn child. Wringing her hands together, she turned and began to leave. This was it. The moment she left this room, she wouldn't be able to ever let Blaine be part of her life. He'd promised her the world, and instead he'd turned hers upside down. Why couldn't he have just left her alone? If he'd left her alone she wouldn't be walking out of a clubhouse feeling like the biggest fool in the world.

"What are you doing here?" Lash asked.

She knew who he was. The whole town of Fort Wills knew who The Skulls were.

"I'm just leaving."

"You shouldn't let him treat you like that," Lash said.

Glancing behind her shoulder, she was struck by pain as Blaine pulled the other woman onto his lap. From where she stood, she saw he was rubbing his dick against her ass. Emily was going to have to see if she'd contracted anything from him as well. It was just another thing to add to the list she needed to see her doctor about. Being heavily pregnant wasn't the best experience of her life. She felt tired, ill, fat, ugly, depressed. None of the glowing reports she'd read from other mothers were happening for her. She was never going to have another kid. Her experience of being a mother would start and end with this baby.

"I don't have a choice."

"He doesn't need to be part of your life, Emily." Lash shook his head. "It's not my place to say anything."

She nodded, and the tears finally started to fall. "He's not going to be part of my life anymore." Emily shrugged. "Make sure he doesn't hurt himself or do anything stupid."

"I will."

Leaving the club behind, along with the man she'd been in love with for so long, Emily knew she was making the right decision. It felt like a weight had been lifted off her shoulders and she'd not been this relieved in so long. She made a promise to herself that no matter what happened in her life, she'd never allow herself to love so freely again. With Blaine, she'd never held anything back. She'd given him everything that she was, and he'd thrown everything in her face. The best way to keep her heart intact was to keep everyone else out. Blaine wasn't the marrying type, or the fathering type. Pressing a hand to her stomach, she smiled. "It's just you and me, sweetheart. You are the only person I need to love."

He didn't even know it was a little girl. Blaine hadn't been there for the scans. He'd not even remembered she had an appointment. Not once had he asked her how it went or what they were having. His lack of interest should have warned her. Driving toward their small apartment, she let herself inside. Their small place was immaculately clean. She liked cleaning, as it took her mind off everything that was about to happen in her crazy world.

Typing her parents' number into her cell phone, she perched on the sofa, and waited.

"Hello," her father, Lenard, said.

Licking her suddenly dry lips, Emily found it hard to talk, yet forced herself to speak. "Hey, Daddy, it's me, Emily."

"Honey, what's wrong?"

"It's, erm, it's not working out. I'm going to leave him, but I've got nowhere else to go. Can I come back home?" She'd disappointed all of them when she went with Blaine. They'd not kicked her out. She had left with Blaine believing she was starting a new life together.

"Baby, you could come back home whenever you want. We miss you."

"I've got to pack a few things. Can I come tonight?"

"Yes. Do you need me to come pick you up?"

"What's going on, Lenard?" She heard her mother in the background. Shirley had tried to stop her leaving. Not once did Emily listen. She wasn't going to do this again. Her parents were always looking out for her. They had her best interests at heart. Blaine only cared about himself, never about her.

"It's okay, go back to sleep."

"I can drive there. I just didn't want to startle you in case you weren't awake."

"Honey, come home. I'll be up and waiting with your favorite hot chocolate."

"Okay." She disconnected the call, gathered her few meager belongings then took one last look around the apartment. This was supposed to be her life, her future, their happiness. Memories of him laughing, planning, and just being the man she loved flashed through her mind. That was all over. The Blaine who'd taken over was mean, unfaithful, a liar, and a cheat.

Closing the door, she left the past behind.

****

Her mother held her hand as pain filled every part of her body. One week late her daughter had decided to finally come into the world. Emily's heart pounded inside her chest as she was struck by the undeniable pain.

"He's got to be here, Momma," she said, sobbing. This should be a happy event, but Blaine was nowhere in sight. She'd not seen him in a few months, not since she moved out. The very thought that he didn't care about her filled her with regret. He owned her heart and soul, yet she didn't even register in his mind.

Slowly, as the pain increased and her mother whispered encouraging words, she brought his daughter into the world. Their baby screamed out, and Emily fell instantly in love. She'd done it, given birth to a little girl.

Blowing out a breath, she gave her mother a shaky smile as the nurse brought her to the bed.

"Honey, she's so beautiful," Shirley said.

"I know."

"What are you going to name her?"

Emily paused as she thought about Blaine. He'd always wanted to name their first child whether it was a boy or girl, but the man who'd told her that was not the man she'd last seen or known.

"Darcy, I'm going to name her Darcy." She smiled up at her mother then back to her daughter. "Do you hear that, baby? Do you like the name Darcy?"

In response her daughter opened her eyes, staring back at her.

Yes, her daughter was going to be named Darcy. Emily's father, Lenard, walked into the room. She knew he was proud with the way his gaze lit up when he saw his granddaughter.

****

"Emily, come on. I'm sorry."

Her parents had taken Darcy out for the day to give her a break. It had been six months since she had given birth without this man present. Six months of waking up at night, dealing with sickness, diapers, and she was exhausted. Her parents were her rock. They were always there for her to help out. They hadn't demanded she go out and get a job to help support them. Her father owned several online companies that dealt with distribution. He told her not to worry about money.

"Go away, Blaine," she said.

She had seen him around town. He no longer wore The Skulls jacket, and from the rumors she heard, he'd lost any chance of being a prospect. Emily didn't care. When she'd seen him around town, he'd been making out with several different women. She couldn't even accept a date and he was fucking any number of faceless women. Blowing out a breath, she pushed hair off her face, trying to find the strength to say the words that needed to be said.

"Baby, I know I fucked up."

On the cabinet on the opposite wall her parents had put a picture of her and Darcy in a frame. Her daughter didn't need a man like Blaine in her life. Getting to her feet, Emily wiped away the tears that had started to fall.

Be strong. Be a good mother to Darcy.

Emily pulled back the chain and opened the door. Blaine looked like shit. His face was bruised, and it looked like he'd been in a fight. The white shirt he wore was stained and torn. His jeans were faded and torn like his shirt. He looked like he'd spent a long time on the streets. She kept hold of the door refusing to let him inside.

"What do you want?" she asked, glaring at him.

Seeing him in the flesh reminded her of his complete lack of interest in their daughter's life.

"I know I fucked up. Can I come in and talk?"

"No."

He paused, clearly shocked by her refusal to let him inside.

"Em, stop being a bitch."

"Do you know you've got a daughter?" she asked. "Do you know her name? Her date of birth? How long did it take you to recognize that I wasn't at your apartment?"

"Enough!"

"No, it's not enough. You got me pregnant because the fucking condom broke, Blaine. You told me to trust you that everything would be okay." The tears she couldn't hold down any longer began to fall. "I trusted you, and you were more interested in fucking other women. I gave birth to a beautiful baby girl six months ago. I named her Darcy. She's the best thing I ever did, but this is by far the best thing I'm going to do as her mother." She snagged the picture off the cabinet, opening up. Emily slammed the picture against his chest. "That is the closest you're ever going to come to seeing our daughter. You come around here again I'll call the cops."

She closed and locked the doors, leaning her weight against the wood. Emily stayed still until she heard his footsteps disappearing. Her heart was breaking inside her chest. She was in pain, and she rubbed at where her heart lay. This was what she needed to do to keep her daughter safe. Blaine wouldn't make a good father. She used to believe in second chances, but no more. The only thing that mattered to her was making sure her daughter didn't suffer.

Emily placed the empty picture frame on the cabinet going through to the kitchen.

She'd done the right thing.

Now she only needed to make herself believe she'd done the right thing.

****

Blaine walked down the steps leaving Emily behind. He held the picture of his daughter in his hand. Even as he tried to make himself believe anyone could have fathered that little girl, he knew it was wrong. Emily had been a virgin when he took her, his virgin. There was no way he could ever believe another man had his woman. Emily loved him, or at least, she did love him at some point. Over the last year he'd fucked up. He'd more than fucked up.

The Skulls had kicked him out of the club. He'd started prospecting to them when he found out Emily was pregnant. The partying had gotten wild, and he'd started using hard drugs, and women. He ran a hand down his face as he thought about how quickly he'd fucked up his life. When Tiny had found out he was using they'd tossed him out on the street without a backward glance, ending his days as a prospect. The moment they kicked him out of the club, the women had turned their backs on him. Thinking back to the partying not one of the women had been a regular club whore. Tiny didn't allow any of the brothers or club whores to use drugs in his club. Walking down the street, Blaine made his way toward the end of the road where the bus stop was. This was what his life had become. He'd lost the woman he loved, the club who was going to make his life better, and he wouldn't even get to know his little girl.

He stared down at the picture in his hand of Emily with his little girl. No matter what he tried to say to make up for what he did, he couldn't make any excuses. This was all his fault.

Sitting on the seat in the bus stop, he stared at the graffiti decorating the walls. Tears gathered in his eyes and fell down his cheeks in waves at all that he'd lost. He shouldn't have pushed Emily aside. Blaine hurt all over from doing the shit he'd done to her. When he was around her, she made him a better man, and he'd fucked it all up.

The sound of a motorbike drew his attention toward the road. Lash appeared at the bus stop pushing his glasses up the top of his head. Out of all of the men, Lash was one of the hardest he knew. He hit the most, demanded most of everyone in the club, and not even Nash his brother, got away with shit. The club had to be beyond reproach with Lash.

"Hey, Blaine."

He wiped his eyes, feeling like a pussy for being

caught crying.

"Don't worry about the tears. I heard you lost everything."

Blaine held a picture of his woman and baby up for him to see. Lash whistled.

"Bitch looks like a keeper."

"She is."

"When a man claims a woman and puts his baby in her belly, he should learn to keep his dick in his pants."

"I fucked up, but you don't know what it's like. You fuck every woman you meet."

Lash climbed off his bike, moving to sit beside him. "When I find the woman that's going to be mine, the woman I love regardless of who she is, I won't even look at another woman."

"You don't know that."

"What makes a man great is knowing that what he's got is perfection. You wanted better even though you screwed that woman over."

All of Lash's words were true. Blaine *had* thought he could do better than Emily, but in truth, Emily deserved better than him.

"She'll never forgive me."

"Nope, and that little girl will never call you daddy." Those words hung in the air between them. Blaine didn't know what to make of them. The very thought of having a kid and not being able to see her, filled him with regret. "Unless of course you get yourself cleaned up. Go away, get cleaned up, and then come back. I'll vouch for you with Tiny. You can start over again. It'll mean you're going to be one of the oldest prospects we could have, but we'd also welcome you back home. However, you've got to start it off." Lash pulled a leaflet out of his pocket. "All you've got to do is make the first step."

He took the leaflet from Lash. It was for a rehab clinic. Lash stood, and Blaine watched him climb back on his bike. "You've got nothing left to lose and everything to gain."

Could he do it? Could he turn his life around?

Turning the leaflet over, he wanted to give it a try. Nothing else had worked, so maybe this would.

Chapter One

Present day

Blaine glanced around the clubhouse as Christmas decorations began to go up all around to make use of every spare surface and wall. Eva stood arranging everything, and from what he heard, Chaos Bleeds were pretty much doing the exact same thing. They were all sharing Christmas within their own clubhouse. He was sad to see the two MCs break apart. Blaine liked Devil and the crew, but shit with Gonzalez was just too deep. No one had come out of it for the better, apart from Whizz.

He glanced over toward Whizz and Lacey. Both were wrapped around each other, neither of them kissing, but each had that look of deep yearning on their faces. Envy filled him at the love shining between the two. Whizz deserved the love and happiness that Lacey was going to give him. Both had gotten over so much to be together, and it hadn't stopped them or their love. He thought about Emily.

They were together, but they weren't together-together. It was a strange set-up. He had an apartment in town, owned outright from the money he earned working for The Skulls. Emily and his little girl Darcy lived with him. Blaine wasn't under any illusions. If it hadn't been for Angel, his girls wouldn't be in his life. He didn't doubt it was down to Angel. Lash's woman lived up to her name. Blaine adored her and would do anything to see that she was happy.

"What's got you looking all serious?" Angel asked, coming out from behind him. She carried Anthony on her hip even though the little boy could walk.

"Nothing."

"Are Emily and Darcy coming for the celebrations?"

He gripped the back of his neck trying to ease out the knots that had formed. Emily lived with him, but he knew half of her stuff remained at her folks'. She didn't trust him even after the last few years together. Emily used every excuse to keep her shit at her parents'. With the way he'd treated her years ago, he'd not even bothered to fight her. He put up with whatever she threw his way. Blaine wasn't in any position to fight back. He'd been a complete ass to her, a cheating ass. When he'd been shot, she'd been by his side, but still she kept him at arms' length. He knew she was afraid to commit to him.

"Yeah, I think they're coming."

It would mean Emily would have to share his bed. She'd shared his bed a couple of times without them having sex. She always put a large pillow between them. Emily would not let him touch her. He couldn't blame her. When he was high on the drugs, he couldn't remember half the shit he'd done. Once the drugs wore off and Emily wasn't around, he'd lost it, sinking deeper into the spiraling pit of hell. Getting clean was the best thing he'd done in a long time. The only problem was knowing he couldn't get close enough to Emily to gain her trust or forgiveness. He talked with her parents, and they didn't have a clue as to how to help him. They had tried talking to her to reason with her and still nothing.

Angel squealed pulling him out of his mundane thoughts. "This is going to be so amazing. A wedding, Christmas, family, it's all coming together." She pulled him in for a hug while still holding Anthony.

Barely a second passed before Lash was tugging his wife into his arms. "Honey, you're going to have to let Anthony go. Our son is getting squashed, and you know I hate it when you let another man hug you."

"Blaine's my friend."

"He's still got a dick."

"It doesn't count."

Blaine chuckled. "I'm going to head out. I've got a few presents still to get." He said his goodbyes on the way out of the shop, heading into town on his bike. It was fucking freezing, and the snow had already laid a nice white blanket over the paths. A snow plow had cleared most of the roads, but in a few days driving would be hazardous for anyone who tried it. He went into the little toy shop that had opened up. All of The Skulls loved it and had bought plenty of gifts for their kids from the store owner, Millie.

"Hey, Blaine. I've got your orders ready," she said, appearing from behind the counter. Millie was a young woman, twenty-five he believed. She was rounded, charming, and sweet. He wouldn't have a bad thing said about her as Emily adored her.

He pulled out his wallet.

"You don't need to do that. Emily stopped by to pay for it all. I got talking to her about your orders for Darcy."

Blaine gritted his teeth to keep from biting out. He truly thought Emily and Darcy had been struggling to live while he'd been doping up on drugs and shit. Her parents were wealthy and had seen to their care. Emily never made him believe anything, but while he'd been in rehab, he'd made himself believe that lie to get him through. The only truth he had was he'd abandoned his woman when she needed him most. She shouldn't have had to rely on her parents.

He'd told Emily he would look after her, had sworn to love and protect her, and he'd failed her so completely.

"I'll just take the gifts then."

"I'm really sorry. I shouldn't have mentioned anything."

"It doesn't matter."

This was Emily pulling away again. Every time he thought they were getting closer, she always pulled back. He hated it.

Leaving the shop with his sack full of presents, he headed toward the café in town. He ordered himself a sandwich and a strong coffee. Blaine stared at the chair beside him. There were a lot of presents. He could take them back to the clubhouse before heading to his apartment or he could take them home with him.

"Hey, Blaine."

He looked up to see Lenard, Emily's father, taking a seat opposite him. It looked like the older man also had a sandwich and coffee.

"Hello, Lenard." They'd stopped being formal a long time ago. Lenard demanded that he treat him like a friend.

"You got the gifts?"

"Emily already paid for them." Blaine shook his head, forcing a smile. "Shit, sorry, I shouldn't have said anything."

"She still giving you a hard time?"

"No, she doesn't give me a hard time. She just doesn't allow herself to depend on me." He picked up his coffee taking a sip. "I deserve it. I didn't exactly give her any reason to trust me." Blaine had come a long way with Lenard. The first time he dated Emily, Lenard had tried everything he could to stop them being together, threatened anything he could think of. Now, Blaine had done everything he could to prove to Emily and her family that he wasn't going to screw up.

It was strange really. Her parents believed him whereas Emily didn't.

"I love my daughter, Blaine. She means the world to me. I know she loves you."

Blaine stared down into his cup unable to take the sincerity in Lenard's eyes. There was a time he'd have believed him. Not anymore. He doubted Emily loved him. Blaine truly believed she only put up with him because of Darcy.

He loved her. There was no denying his love for her, but he'd begun to doubt her feelings for him. Blaine had bought her a ring over a year ago, not long after he'd gotten shot. He'd heard her calling to him. At the time he couldn't explain it, was afraid to even understand what was going on. Then he was awake and the first thing he'd seen coming out of the coma he'd been in was Emily's tear filled eyes. Seeing her face and, more importantly, the expression on her face kept him believing they still had a chance to be together. He'd hurt her badly all those years ago. It was almost impossible to break through the ice she kept between them, but Blaine couldn't walk away. He loved her too damn much.

"What if you're wrong?" He couldn't keep holding onto the past.

"Emily's a stubborn woman, like her mother. When she wants something or loves someone, she gives all of herself. There's no holding back with her. When she gave her heart to you, Blaine, she gave it all to you. She's hurt, and she's scared."

"I've proven to her that I'm going to be there."

"But you're not fighting her. You're giving her a chance to have these doubts without being the Blaine she knew and loved. You've become complacent, almost worried in your approach to her. Your skittishness is what's making her have doubts. You don't show any confidence in yourself anymore. Why should she trust you? For all Emily knows, you're scared about going back to the way things were." Lenard stopped talking to take a drink. "Don't get me wrong. You broke my little girl's heart, and I wanted to fucking kill you, ten times over. I thought about it, planned it, I was fucking ready for it, but I knew she'd be more heartbroken to never see you again than anything else. Don't give up on my girl otherwise I'd have to kill you." Lenard finished off his coffee. "I better be getting back. Shirley hates it when I'm late for dinner."

Blaine watched him leave the café. Sitting back, he let out a sigh. He was well and truly fucked as he didn't know what to do. The last thing he wanted to do was push Emily away. She was his life, his reason for living. He couldn't lose her.

****

"You've got to give that boy a chance," Shirley said, stirring her sauce as Emily threw in the herbs. They cooked together as Darcy did her homework at the kitchen counter. Emily glanced over at her daughter to see her listening to music with her headphones on. Darcy was now five years old, in full-time school, and growing faster than Emily liked to think about. It wouldn't be long before she had posters of guys on her wall, talking about boys, and leaving for college.

Get a grip, Emily.

"Could we not talk about this?"

"It's all we need to talk about. Blaine is a good man."

"Mom, I live with him—"

"Honey, stop acting dumb. It doesn't do you any favors. You're not really living with Blaine. All you're doing is waiting for the boy to screw up. It has been three years, maybe even more. He's been there for Darcy and

23

you."

Emily closed her eyes. She hated listening to this.

"You're supposed to be agreeing with me. I'm doing the right thing." She rubbed at her temples as a headache started to begin.

"No, you're stopping yourself from having fun, and that includes that boy of yours."

"Blaine's not a boy."

"You've got to start thinking about Darcy. Maybe a little brother or sister? It would be good for everyone."

Emily blew out a breath as she threw in the last of the torn up basil. Her parents had been doing nothing but talking to her constantly about Blaine. They liked this new side of him.

I like this new side of him.

The last couple of years had been a rollercoaster ride of happiness, fear, excitement, and disappointment. Blaine, the boy she had fallen in love with, was still there. She saw the real man in his eyes when he allowed himself to relax enough around her. The moments were fleeting but there. He was always nervous. Was he scared about using again? Did he think about drugs all the time while he was with her? Did he want the other women he used to be with?

She'd not been with anyone but Blaine. The last time they'd had sex was a few months before Darcy was born. Surely he'd been with another woman. Emily had urges all the time and had come close to giving in, but then she'd sense this unease, and she'd lose all confidence in herself. Had Blaine been with another woman since they'd moved in together? She'd not seen him with another woman.

Great, she was losing her mind now thinking about Blaine with another woman.

"Finished," Darcy said slamming her book

closed, and removing her headphones.

"Go watch some cartoons, darling," Shirley said.

"Sure thing, Grandma."

Darcy left the room leaving her alone with her mother.

She turned to face her mother and groaned. The determined look on her face didn't bode well for Emily.

"Mom, don't."

"Women have needs as much as men. You're in love with Blaine, always have been. I'm not going to watch you destroy yourself yearning for a man—"

"He's not even mine!"

"Don't interrupt me, little miss. I get that he hurt you. I understand it, but it has been years. He's not fucked up yet, has he?"

Emily didn't answer, feeling like a petulant child for not doing it.

"Emily, answer me."

"No, he hasn't."

"Go home. Spend some time alone with Blaine without Darcy. Your father and I love having Darcy around."

"It's okay. I can take Darcy with m—"

"I'm trying to tell you to go and get that man laid." Her mother's cheeks turned a bright red. Emily's heated at her mother trying to get her to sleep with Blaine.

"Mom?"

"I may be your mother, but I'm still a woman. You were not born through a Virgin Birth. I love your father, and so did a lot of other women at the time. I made sure he didn't have a reason to go hunting for another woman. The trick to keeping your man happy is being everything he needs so he doesn't go looking elsewhere."

"You're saying I failed Blaine all those years ago?" Emily asked, hurt by her mother's outburst.

"No. Blaine was a complete asshole back then. He was too young and a blithering idiot. He let you down and he let us down, but now he's trying and has been trying for a long time."

"You should be on my side."

"I am, honey. He was and still is the love of your life. I know and you know you're just scared in case he ruins it again. I can tell you Blaine is not going to ruin it. He loves you."

Emily didn't say anything. Hope flared inside her, but at the same time it ended as she recalled all the women hanging off him.

You've got to stop thinking about this.

She really wanted to forget about the past, but it was too hard to do. The last time she gave herself to Blaine he'd torn her heart out and stamped on it. Could she allow herself to give herself back to him?

"We're looking after Darcy tonight. Go, have some fun with Blaine. Besides, I've not made enough for you anyway."

"Mom!"

"Don't 'mom' me. You've got needs, and you seriously need to relax. I look at you and I tense up." Shirley walked over to her, cupping her cheek. "You've got to relax, honey. From what I hear Blaine has already beaten himself up enough over what happened with you and the baby."

"He saw me, Mom. He came by the house when you and Dad were out. I showed him a picture of Darcy. He knows we were fine."

Shirley wrapped her arms around her. "You ever thought that thinking the worst is what got him by? Men do stupid things, but he came back for you, Emily. Blaine has always come back for you. Think about that when the worst of the memories are threatening to spill over."

She held her mother tightly then released her going to find her daughter. As she walked down the hall her father entered the house.

"Hey, honey."

"Hey, Daddy." She hugged him tight, glancing to the left to see Darcy sitting beautifully in front of the television. Emily loved that little girl, and she really wanted the best for her.

"I bumped into Blaine. He had a lot of presents, and he looked pretty bummed."

Heat filled her cheeks once again. Millie had let slip that Blaine had spent a fortune on presents. She couldn't bring herself to let him pay for all of them.

"Emily, you're giving him a hard time."

"You as well. You're my parents and should be agreeing with me." She pressed a hand to her chest.

"I do agree with you. I agreed with you three years ago when he first came back into your life. Three years, Em, has he given you any reason to doubt him?"

"No."

"Then stop being stubborn and stop fighting him. It won't do you any good."

"I'm going to go home. Mom's kicking me out." She hugged her father close then entered the sitting room. Darcy climbed onto her lap.

"I love you, Mommy."

"I love you, too, baby." She kissed Darcy's head, breathing in her scent. Whenever she thought about Blaine in the past and the pain threatened to claw her alive, she always hugged her daughter. Darcy made everything better for her.

Shirley cleared her throat.

"I'm going, I'm going."

Darcy chuckled. "Give Daddy a hug from me."

"I will, honey."

She stroked Darcy's hair then turned to leave. "I'm going, Mom."

"Good. Go and have some fun."

Leaving the safety of her parents' house she made her way out into the cold. She'd walked all the way and so she needed to make the trek back home. Emily thought about Christmas. Blaine had mentioned spending the week at the clubhouse. Every Christmas she spent with her parents. Would they hate not having them over at Christmas? She'd need to talk to her parents about it.

If they wanted her and Darcy for Christmas then she wouldn't go to the clubhouse.

That's cruel.

Tears filled her eyes, and she let out a breath. She thought about her parents' advice. Should she give Blaine a chance? Hadn't she already given him a chance? They were living together.

Are you really?

She and Darcy still had a room at her parents'.

No, she'd not given Blaine a chance. She was always ready to leave at a moment's notice.

Emily stared down at the snow as guilt swamped her. She had been unfair to Blaine from the beginning. The fear of what he had done to her in the past had been at the forefront of her mind. She wouldn't give him a chance, and for three long, miserable years, she'd made him pay.

By the time she made it back to their apartment building she was freezing. Entering the building she saw the fake blonde who lived down the hall from them. Nicole, she believed her name was.

"Hello, Emily," Nicole said. "Where's Blaine? I've not seen him for quite some time."

"I don't know."

"He's so yummy. I wouldn't let him go if I was you. You know what they say about The Skulls?"

Emily stood, staring at the woman. Nicole was everything she wasn't, slender with large fake tits. Her own breasts were large, but they also held the memory of carrying a child. She had stretch marks and an added layer of thickness to her body. Above everything, Nicole was fun. She could see it in Nicole's eyes. Any man who took a turn with Nicole wouldn't be left unsatisfied.

"No, what do they say?"

"Once you've had a Skull there's no turning back. It's why they've got a club full of women. There's no way you can leave them."

Feeling sick, Emily made her way toward the stairs. "I better get home."

"Tell Blaine hi."

Nodding, she walked up the long flight of stairs. She pulled her key out of her pocket then entered their shared apartment. Blaine lived in a good part of town, not that there were many bad parts with The Skulls present. They made sure everything stayed above board. The scent of garlic met her senses.

She closed the door, removing her coat as Blaine appeared around the corner. He only wore a short sleeved shirt, and she saw the ink that decorated his arms.

"Hey," he said. "Where's Darcy?"

"Spending the night at my parents'. They wouldn't let me bring her home." She walked down the hall going toward him. In her mind flashed a memory of their last apartment. When he'd entered during their first few weeks together, she'd run toward him. Blaine would open him arms out to embrace her.

This hadn't happened in such a long time. She stopped several feet from him. "Nicole told me to tell you hi."

"Who's Nicole?"

"Fake blonde with big tits?"

Blaine frowned. "Sorry, haven't got a clue."

"I'm sure she'll be disappointed." Emily stared at his lips, wishing there was something else she could say to him. Instead, she looked toward the kitchen.

"What you got cooking?"

"Erm, a curry, I think."

She walked into the kitchen to find a curry bubbling on the stove. Lifting the lid on another pan, she saw fluffy rice.

"This smells amazing."

He leaned against the doorframe, watching her. Emily licked her suddenly dry lips. It took every ounce of control not to go to him.

Would it hurt?

"I picked up the presents from Millie today."

"Yeah."

"Why did you go and pay for them?"

She tucked some hair behind her ear. There was no getting away from the guilt now. When she'd paid for them she'd truly believed she was doing a good thing. Now, she no longer believed so.

"I didn't want you to be out of pocket. Those toys cost a lot of money."

Chapter Two

"Darcy's my daughter as well. I like buying shit for her, Emily." Blaine was losing his temper. When she'd walked into the apartment toward him, he'd known she was thinking about the times when they were younger. He'd loved coming home just to have her running toward him. Blaine missed her being open with her affection. She wouldn't give him a little leeway. He thought about Lenard's advice. Maybe it was time to start pushing a little more. He wasn't going to leave or start using drugs nor was he going to screw around with other women.

The fact she mentioned Nicole only told him she was waiting for him to screw up. He didn't know who the bitch was, but whoever she was had left Emily feeling sad.

"I know."

"If you know why didn't you let me pay for them? You've already bought Darcy gifts. I've seen them stuffed in the wardrobe, Em."

She turned to look at him, folding her arms underneath her breasts. The jeans she wore molded to her curves, but the shirt was so big he couldn't even make the outline of her body. He'd noticed this about his woman, that she rarely let herself be seen. They shared a bed, but again she wore large pajamas. Didn't she realize he only needed to be in her company to be turned on? This was what he had to live with from the moment he first met her. There was a four year age gap between them, and he'd met her by chance when he'd gone to a bonfire and the high school kids had joined. At the time he'd been working at the coffee shop as he'd not made the grades to go to college. He'd been trying to get an apprentice position at The Skulls' mechanic shop, which he'd failed to get as they were fully staffed. Blaine had looked toward the lake to find one woman standing on her own.

Blaine couldn't even describe what happened to him, but he'd needed to drag himself toward her. She had pulled him close, and it hadn't changed after all this time. He found himself meeting up with her after school just to be close to her. Over the course of another few weeks, he'd fallen in love with her. He never pressured her to have sex, and they both waited until she was eighteen. When they were together, he'd promised to take care of her, protect her, look after her. The condom had split on him, and she'd become pregnant.

Their life hadn't turned out like he hoped. His plans had gotten caught up in his own stupid shit.

"I'm sorry."

"Are you really sorry?"

"Yes."

"I don't know, Emily. What more do I have to do to prove to you I'm not going to let you down. I'm here to stay to be your man and a father to Darcy."

"I don't want you to be my man. I only want you to be a father to our daughter."

He closed the distance between them, angered at her complete lack of care when it came to him. "You don't want me." He reached out to grip her waist. "I've done everything you've asked me to. I've not touched you or pressured you to be with me." With one hand on her waist, he cupped her cheek. "I have deserved half the crap you've dished out to me for the way I treated you before, but don't think you can tell me I'm not your man. It's time you trusted me completely, Em."

Blaine slammed his lips down on hers, moaning as she opened up to him. Emily gripped both of his arms, but he didn't break away from the kiss. It had been too long since he'd had her in his arms, tasting her, loving her. He felt like he'd been drowning and could finally breathe with her in his arms. There was no way he was letting her go. Blaine knew he couldn't let her go. She meant too much to him to allow her to leave again.

Sliding his tongue over her lips, he pressed inside to meet her tongue. Emily tightened her grip on his arms yet didn't push him away. He gripped her hair, tilting her head back so that he could deepen the kiss.

She released a moan, and he broke the kiss long enough to look into her eyes, which were dilated and full of arousal.

"Blaine?"

Her voice was croaky, and it went straight to his cock. This was the woman he'd been missing for so long.

"Don't ever say I'm not your man. I'm your man, Emily, and have been from the first moment I saw you. If any man tries to touch you, I'll fucking kill them."

"Don't—"

He cut her off by slamming his lips down on hers. She melted against him, and he loved it. Blaine relished the feel of her pressed against him.

"No, this shit that's going on between us. It ends. I understand I fucked up, but I'm proving to you I'm not going to hurt you. I love you, Emily. Always have, always will. I'll buy shit for Darcy and for you without you paying for the crap." He stroked her cheek, loving the feel of her against his fingers. "I'm not going to let you do this to us any longer. I've done everything you asked. I'm not going to change."

"I'm scared."

Her eyes filled with tears, breaking his heart to know it was his fault. "I'm here. You can be scared all you want, but you've got to know that I'm here for you.

I'll catch you when you fall. I'll be the one you'll be screaming for when you're coming. Me, Emily. I'm not backing down or leaving."

He wiped the tears away as they started to fall.

"No more tears, Emily. Trust me. I won't let you down." He dropped another kiss to her lips. "Go and have a bath, relax. We'll have some food."

Emily nodded.

Releasing her, he watched her walk toward their room. They had an en-suite bathroom so she had time away from Darcy. When he'd bought the place he'd done so with Emily's comfort in mind.

He gave the curry another quick stir then made his way toward the table he'd started to set before she came in. Checking the table, he then grabbed his cell phone to dial Lenard.

"She's not on her way here, is she?" Lenard asked.

"No. We're making progress. Small progress but it's better than nothing. I'm calling about Christmas. The Skulls are having a get-together at the club. Do you want Emily and Darcy around for Christmas?"

Silence met his question.

"Tell him, Lenard," Shirley said.

He must be on speakerphone.

"We've booked ourselves a cruise for Christmas. We leave a week before Christmas and don't come back until the New Year. Shirley and I were talking, and we believe that we have intervened too much. It's time for Emily to stand on her own two feet. We've put off going away on a cruise as we felt she needed us all the time. This year it's time for her to be with you and Darcy."

Blaine let out a breath. "Do you want me to tell her?"

"No. We'll be talking to her about it when she

comes for Darcy. I'm putting trust into you, Blaine. You're the only man who can make her happy. I'm sure of it."

He mumbled his agreement, not sure if he completely agreed with her parents. Blaine ended the call just as Emily walked through the door. She was dressed in a skirt that went to her ankles along with another of those long, shapeless shirts. He needed to get her in clothes that made her feel sexy or at the very least, like a woman.

"Take a seat." He pulled a chair out, waiting for her to take a seat. She hesitated for a split second before taking a seat. Blaine leaned forward, moving her raven hair out of the way. He dropped a kiss to her neck, wanting to do a hell of a lot more but holding off. There would be time for that soon. "I'll get food."

Blaine turned the stove off, and served them both plenty of food. He walked back to the table, taking a seat across from her.

She picked up her fork, and he noticed her hand shook a little. He'd kissed her, and he wanted her to get used to having him touch her. Angel had brought Emily back into his life. He wondered if he could ask her help in winning back his woman.

No one at the club knew the truth about his relationship with Emily. They all thought they were a couple even though they were the furthest thing from a couple. He thought about Angel with Lash, Eva and Tiny, even Whizz and Lacey—they were all united couples. No one could tear them apart even if they tried. That's what he wanted for them, and he would make sure they had it.

****

The curry was everything she loved, spicy, delicious, and his specialty. Emily bit into a chunk of chicken moaning as the taste exploded on her tongue. She'd always loved Blaine's cooking. They both shared a passion for good food.

"This is really good," she said.

Her hand kept shaking, which she hated. The bath was supposed to have made her relax, not driven her even crazier. Then he'd gone and kissed her on the neck. All it had done was remind her of the times Blaine wouldn't stop kissing her. They had been together a year before they had sex. Blaine had been the perfect gentleman, waiting for her to be of age before taking the next step. When he'd taken her virginity, they hadn't held back. She loved being with him, even though the sex hadn't been earth shattering. The earth shattering sex had come a good deal after. She'd not been with another man but Blaine. Even though they'd been over she couldn't bring herself to be with another man. She hadn't wanted to taint the memory she had of Blaine with another man.

"I live to serve." He reached between them, resting his hand on top of hers.

The kiss they'd shared had set her pulse racing and heat flooding her pussy. She couldn't fight the memories with him this close. It was too hard. Emily didn't move her hand away even though she knew she should. If she wanted to keep her distance, she had to create some space between them.

"Will you come to the clubhouse tomorrow? They're putting up all the decorations. You won't believe how different it looks. Tiny's let his woman loose on the place."

Emily laughed. Eva, Angel, and Kelsey were wonderful women. She didn't get on well with Tate, but the others were okay. "What about Darcy?"

"We can pick her up afterward."

SAM CRESCENT

"Okay. It should be fun."

She looked down at her food as Blaine squeezed her hand. Glancing at their hands, she felt a shard of pain through her heart.

You've got to stop pushing him away.

"You always used to love Christmas," he said. "I remember how you dragged me around every fairy light and tree display."

He was talking about the time when she was still in high school. She wouldn't let him put a downer on the season. Emily recalled making sugar cookies for him, brownies, inviting him back home to meet her parents.

Shirley and Lenard had been pleasant to him, but once he'd left their home for the night, both had voiced their concerns about his age. She'd brushed aside their concern.

They're not concerned anymore.

No. They weren't concerned anymore. In fact they were trying to get her married off to him already.

"I still love Christmas."

"Then why haven't you put your own touch to this place?"

She looked up at him to find him staring intently back at her. "What do you mean?"

"Everyone has decorated for Christmas, yet this place looks the same. The only sense of Christmas is Darcy's Advent calendar in the hallway by the door."

Emily twirled her fork on her plate. She'd been tempted to decorate their apartment. Like with everything else she'd held herself back, refusing to take that next step.

"I didn't know it's what you wanted."

"This is your place as well."

She looked around the space.

"You've not even made an effort to put your own

37

mark on the place," he said.

"I, erm, I thought it looked great without anything else added to it. I didn't want to spoil your, I mean, our space."

He dropped his fork to the half empty plate. "You're still waiting for me to fail, aren't you?"

"No." She didn't sound convincing even to herself. "Look, I didn't know what you wanted."

"Our first apartment was in a shithole. It was awful, and yet you still got your hands stuck in making it ours. This is our apartment, Emily."

She opened her mouth, then closed it. There was no point in arguing. Everything he said was right while she was wrong. "I'll decorate."

Blaine stood, taking his plate from the table.

Her appetite gone, she carried her plate into the kitchen. She froze as she watched him throw his plate into the sink. Emily heard it shatter on impact.

"This is going to stop," Blaine said.

She held onto her plate tightly as he gripped the counter by the sink. Staring at his knuckles she saw they were white from where he held onto the sink.

"I've not done anything wrong." *Is what I've done really acceptable?* Emily didn't like the way she was feeling. She *was* in the wrong. For three years she'd been doing this, but was it okay for her to do this? Her parents believed she needed to move on. She no longer knew what to do.

"No. You never did anything wrong. I did, and you can't bring yourself to forgive me, can you?"

He spun around, his dark eyes staring back at her. She shivered at being assessed by him. Blaine stared at her, yet he saw a lot more than she wanted him to see.

"You were by my side when I was shot. You're always there for me, Emily. Every time I think we're moving forward, you hold yourself back. Do you even love me anymore?"

Tears filled her eyes once again. She couldn't look at him and stared down at her plate, hoping like so many other times that he would give up. Blaine wasn't the man she once knew. The man from her past before he succumbed to drugs and drink wouldn't let her hide. This man in front of her was always hesitant around her. She hated it, and she hated the man he'd become. When she visited the club to see him, they all got the Blaine she'd once loved. She didn't. She got a shell of the man, but had she really encouraged him to move on?

What kind of woman was she to be envious of a club?

"No, you don't get to hide from me anymore." He stepped closer, taking the plate from her. She tried to hold onto the plate, but he tore it from her grip.

"Will you stop?"

"No, you're going to answer me. I'm tired of this bullshit, Em. When I kissed you, you wanted me. You kissed me back. This woman, this isn't you, and this isn't me. We're hurting Darcy this way."

"Do you think I don't know that?" she asked, crying out.

"Answer my question."

"No."

He gripped her arms, pulling her close. "Stop torturing us and answer my goddamn question, Em. Do you love me or not?"

She stared into his eyes and sobbed. "I don't know."

The moment she spoke the words, she felt a part of herself break apart. She pressed her hands to her face. Emily sobbed into her hands, wishing she could take back the last couple of minutes of arguing.

Blaine released her. "Have you been with another man?"

"What?" she asked, looking up at him.

"The woman I knew wouldn't be like this."

"Blaine, we're different."

"For the last three years we've been together. We're not different."

"We are. You're not the same man you used to be."

He let her go. "Is there another man?"

She glanced down to see his hands were fisted. His earlier threat passed through her mind. "No, there's isn't another man." He relaxed slightly at her words.

"I'm sorry for losing my temper. I shouldn't have hurt you." He reached out to rub her arms. Didn't he realize he'd not even held her roughly?

There was no pain from his touch. Emily was in pain because of her own stupidity.

"I suggest you go and watch some television." Blaine turned away from her once again. This was what she hated. Their arguing only created more of a distance.

Isn't this what you wanted?

Emily truly didn't know. She watched him clean away the plate he'd smashed.

What could she say to him?

She didn't know how to reach out to the man she'd fallen in love with. Turning away, she walked into the sitting room. She curled up on the sofa, grabbing the remote. Flicking through the channels, she felt cold. Emily wrapped a blanket around her, trying to get warm. Nothing helped. She was cold to the bone, and the only person she'd ever wanted to warm her up was gone.

They were only torturing themselves with this cold between them. She didn't know how to stop her reactions nor did she know how to reach out and touch him.

****

"What do you think?" Whizz asked, moving behind Lacey as she stared at the main room of the clubhouse. She looked so beautiful, and he'd recently dyed her hair a deep purple. They needed to wait for the blue to run out before she'd let him. The brothers kept talking smack to him for dying his woman's hair. Whizz didn't care. This was part of their relationship, a development he'd been looking forward to.

"It's beautiful."

"This is all for you."

"Liar. You didn't do this at all." She turned in his arms, and he pulled her close.

"Well, I would have done it if you wanted."

She laughed, shaking her head. "You're a terrible liar. Eva and Angel did amazing. Baker, Ink, and Fighter helped."

"Are they looking to be voted in soon?"

"I don't know. Tiny's finishing up the building work on the town hall. He's also arranging a Christmas fair for the town folk."

"Christmas fair?"

"Yeah, it's a gathering for Fort Wills. We all go, have some fun, alcohol, Christmas. It's like a summer fair only Christmasey."

"It sounds wonderful."

"We'll be going as well." He pressed a kiss to her plump lips. His cock hardened as she snuggled closer against him, kissing him back.

"I love you, Whizz."

Joy filled him. He didn't know what he'd done to deserve her. They'd come a long way together. He still preferred to be cuffed to their bed at night. The last time he'd not been cuffed and one of his nightmares had affected him, he'd almost killed Lacey. He still remembered the red marks that had dotted her neck because of him. Whizz would take every single precaution necessary.

"I love you, Lacey."

He was going to be married to her soon. Whizz had set everything in motion. The club knew he was going to marry her, and so did Lacey. At first, he was going to make it a surprise event but then decided against it. He wanted Lacey involved every step of the way. In the beginning the club hadn't wanted anything to do with her because of her connections to the Savage Brothers MC. The Skulls had to live with his ultimatum. It hadn't been an empty threat. He didn't know what he would have done if they'd not accepted Lacey. She was the love of his life.

Sinking his fingers into her hair, he tilted her head back. "It's time for bed. I need to fuck you again."

Whizz hadn't told her about the appointment he'd made with an adoption agency. He wanted to find out their chances of adopting before he allowed her to get her hopes up. Whizz wasn't going to let Lacey be hurt again. He'd find a way for them to have children.

Chapter Three

Blaine woke up the following morning and stared at Emily. There wasn't a pillow between them, just her ugly ass pajamas that kept him away from her. She better enjoy the peace for now. He wasn't going to let her put up this wall between them. Last night he'd lost his temper, but her response had given him something to think about. She didn't know if she loved him anymore.

Reaching out, he tucked some hair behind her ear. She snuggled against the bed. One of her hands was flat on the bed between them.

He stroked a finger down her cute button nose. Slowly, she started to stir and open her eyes. Blaine smiled.

"Morning, baby," he said.

She smiled back up at him. "Morning." She stretched out her body, groaning as she did. With her back arched Blaine got a perfect view of her nice full tits. Her nipples were rock hard as he'd turned the heating off that night before going to bed. The apartment was cold but worth it. If Darcy had been home, he'd have kept it on.

This was totally worth it. His mouth watered, and all he wanted to do was touch her.

Do it. Be the man she needs you to be.

Without doubting his actions, he placed a hand on her hip, sliding his fingers under her shirt.

"Blaine?"

He didn't speak. She didn't stop him as he moved his hand up over her ribcage. Staring into her eyes he watched her reaction as he cupped her naked breast. They were fuller than he remembered.

"Did you breastfeed Darcy?"

"Yes."

This was what he loved about Emily. She was a natural woman. There was nothing fake about her. Lenard was right. She loved with her whole heart. Emily never gave half. It was always full. But she was giving him half of herself. She was scared to give herself completely, and he'd been the one to destroy that part of her. He'd make sure she didn't have a choice but to love him.

He removed his hand long enough to open the buttons on her pajama shirt. Blaine revealed her tits to his gaze. They were large, full, and the tips of her nipples were rock hard.

"Beautiful," he said, stroking a thumb over one hard bud.

"Blaine?"

"I've been thinking about seeing you like this for a long time." He leaned in close, flicking the tip of her dark red nipple with his tongue.

They both groaned. The sound filled the air between them, echoing off the walls.

He sucked the nipple into his mouth as he pinched the other. Blaine flicked the tip a final time before moving toward the other. He slid his hands down her body to rest on her pajama bottoms. His cock was rock hard, and he wore a pair of sweat pants that didn't hide his raging erection.

"Please, Blaine."

"Don't worry, baby. I've got you covered. I'm going to make you feel so good." He went to his knees and started to remove her pants. Within seconds he had her completely naked. Leaving the bed, he tugged his sweat pants off. He wouldn't fuck her this morning. The only time he'd fuck her was when she was begging him to do it.

Crawling on the bed, he opened her thighs, seeing the fight in her eyes.

He didn't give her a chance to push him away.

Blaine opened the lips of her sex, pressing his thumb to her clit.

She arched up. Her tits shook with her indrawn breath.

"Are you as juicy as I remember?"

He closed the distance between them, opening her pussy to see her swollen clit. She was soaking wet. His mouth watered, and he didn't wait for her permission. Blaine sucked her nub, groaning as her cream filled his mouth.

"Blaine." She screamed his name, thrusting her pelvis up against him.

"So wet and so juicy." He moved down to her entrance and pressed his tongue inside. She tasted musky, sweet, and exactly like his woman. "You're perfect."

"Please, Blaine."

"Do you want me to make you come?"

"Yes. Please, Blaine, I need it. I've not been with anyone else but you. I need you."

He was going to be everything to her. Blaine wasn't going to walk away. She may not know what she felt for him, but he wasn't going to let her doubt her feelings for him again. He didn't go through all the shit he went through just to lose her now. She was his woman, and he wasn't going to let her get away.

Plundering her cunt with his tongue, he stroked her clit. Her screams grew louder as he teased her pussy.

"This is my pussy, Emily. I took your virginity. I lay claim to it. You gave birth to my child. The only dick this cunt will ever see is mine."

She moaned.

"Tell me."

"It's only going to be yours. All yours."

His cock leaked pre-cum, but he refused to touch himself. The last few years he'd found his release by his own hand with memories of Emily. She was the only woman who could make him feel like this.

"Please, Blaine."

Pulling away, he left her hanging.

"What?"

"You'll get your orgasm but only when I'm good and ready." He moved over her, looking down into her beautiful blue eyes. Blaine felt himself falling like he always did into their depth. She was all his.

Gripping his naked cock, he glided the length between the lips of her pussy. She was so soaking wet that they didn't need any lube to help him move. Her cream coated the whole of his length.

"What are you doing?"

"I'm going to deal with that ache we've both got." He doubted Emily had even touched herself since their time together. She wouldn't have found release as she'd always been hesitant about doing so when they were together.

He took hold of both of her hands and pressed them on either side of her head.

"I'm going to make you feel so good." Blaine claimed her lips as he began to thrust between her pussy lips. He bumped her clit and when he looked into her eyes, he saw the pleasure consume her. In that moment, Blaine knew he was right. She'd not had an orgasm in a long time.

It only took three thrusts of his cock and he felt her body tense up. Her cries filled the air, and he watched her, as he pumped between her thighs. After being without her for so long, Blaine followed her into an earth-shattering orgasm, sharing the moment with her as he pulsed his cum onto her stomach. He plunged his tongue into her mouth, kissing her long, and hard.

She tightened her hands around his.

When it was over and the pleasure ebbed away, he pulled back to look at her.

"I'm not going to fuck you until you beg me, but I'm not going to leave you alone anymore, Emily. It hasn't done either of us any good. I want you like I've always wanted you. No more holding back. No more waiting."

"I don't know what you want from me."

"I want you. I've always wanted you."

He kissed her one final time, pulling her into his arms. Blaine carried her through to their shower, turning on the water. They both screamed as they were blasted with cold water.

"It's fucking freezing." She screamed, scrambling to get away. They both burst out laughing, and for the first time in three years, Blaine felt the ice break a little. It wasn't over between them, and if he wasn't careful, they'd go back to the way things were. He was determined not to let that happen.

Blaine picked up the soap, washing her body as she did the same. This was what he'd been wanting. The connection flowed between them. It was still there even if Emily had her doubts. She loved him. He just needed to push her a little harder to prove to her he wasn't going to change.

The man he'd been was not the man she fell in love with. He knew that now. By trying to give her time, he'd only filled her with doubts. It was his mistake that he could easily rectify. The club had his back, and he had a plan.

The Skulls was filled with romantic women who

liked to see a happy ending. It was time he gave Emily their happy ending. He would need Angel to succeed in his plan.

****

Emily couldn't believe the transformation of the club. A large tree with tinsel, baubles, and fairy lights stood tall and proud in the corner, and there was an abundance of gifts already underneath the tree. She watched as Blaine put the gifts she'd stored in their wardrobe underneath the tree. Emily had called her parents asking about Christmas only to be told they'd booked a trip.

After the events of this morning she wasn't sure if she wanted to spend Christmas at the clubhouse. They would be together with no excuse for her to leave, even though part of her didn't want an excuse. Even as she thought about creating a distance between them, she also hated the thought. This morning had been amazing. The feel of his body against her own had been everything she'd missed.

He'd surprised her by the depth of his arousal. If he had spread her thighs open and taken her hard, she wouldn't have protested. She wanted him as much as he wanted her.

"I've got to wrap the gifts I picked up yesterday. We'll bring them with us soon," Blaine said, moving to stand beside her.

"You better hurry. We watched the forecast this morning. It's set to snow and not stop for a good week," Angel said, walking into the room carrying a large cream covered pie.

Emily chuckled as she saw all the men gathered in the room swarm Angel. The blonde woman was known for her cooking, and also her beautiful personality. When she saw the friendship between Angel and Blaine, she'd been a little jealous. Then she'd felt stupid when she saw Lash and Angel together. No one could come between the happy couple. They were both devoted to one another. It was a beautiful sight to witness.

"You greedy bastards better save a slice for me," Lash said, entering the room.

"It's your fault. You shouldn't let her cook." Gash held a plate in his hands looking triumphant. "Score."

It didn't last long as Nash took the plate, charging for the kitchen.

"You greedy fucking bastard."

Chaos ensued as Angel put the pie down and took a step away. She looked a little worried as the men landed blows to one another.

"Okay, I don't think I should make a pie again," Angel said, coming to stand between them.

"They're delicious, Angel. What do you expect?" Blaine asked. Emily jumped as he gripped her shoulders, massaging out the kinks. "You're not cooking your apple pies, Em. I'll kill any bastard who comes near them."

She frowned. Emily hadn't made apple pie in years because … because it was Blaine's favorite. The guilt hit her once again. Her mother had told her it was stupid to stop making something, but she couldn't help it. Blaine had hurt her so much she'd even stopped cooking one of her own favorite pies.

"Apple pie?" Angel asked.

"Yeah, Em makes the best." He pressed a kiss to her temple.

"I'd love to try it. You know what, Emily, with the snow coming I think it would be the perfect time to visit the spa. I love to go, and it sounds like it'll be too dangerous to go later."

"The spa?" Emily asked.

The crowd around the pie dispersed, and Emily saw nothing in the bowl but a crumb.

"Yeah, we could go. I know Lacey's free as well. Whizz wants me to take her out." Angel leaned in close. "He's getting a surprise ready. I'd love the company to help keep her occupied."

"The spa sounds like a good idea," Lash said.

Emily glanced up at Blaine to see he was paying way too much attention to the tree. "What do you think?"

"About what, baby?"

Blaine had set this up. Emily would play along for now.

"About the spa?"

"You deserve a rest. You work too damn hard." He rubbed her shoulders. "It might help you to relax a little more."

"Okay, I'll go," Emily said.

Angel smiled. "Great. I'll get Lacey. This is going to be fun."

Lash followed his woman out of the room.

"What's going on?" Emily asked.

"Nothing. I'll get Darcy, and I'll meet you back at the spa."

"You're up to something. I know you are."

"I'm not." He held his hands up in surrender. "I'm not up to anything. I think it would be good if we spent the night here. Darcy can get used to the club before Christmas."

She didn't see any reason to argue with him.

Within minutes she was packed into a car with Baker driving them all to the spa. Lash joined them, and when they climbed out of the spa in Fort Wills he even walked with them to the main reception.

"I'm going to stay here and wait for you," Lash

said.

"You're always so worried about the worst happening to me." Angel went on her toes and pressed a kiss to his cheek. "What about Anthony?"

"Last time I checked he was spending the afternoon with Tabitha. Eva's got the kids."

"I heard Tabitha got a new friend. She met Daisy at nursery the other week."

Emily listened to the couple talk as they signed in.

"Yeah, but did you hear that Daisy came from the trailer park? Her parents are not great. Eva doesn't like it and has tried to get Tiny to deal with it," Lash said.

"She's a nice kid, quiet. I like Daisy." Angel kissed him again. "Now, it's girl time, so I'm going to leave you, husband."

Lash chuckled, watching his woman go. His gaze landed on Emily seconds later.

"Don't hurt her," he said, warning her.

Emily opened her mouth then closed it. What should she say? She'd had minimum contact with Lash before. She knew he was protective of Angel. The gossip around Fort Wills was rife with rumors. Emily had heard Lash had to be sedated at the hospital when Angel had been shot. She didn't know if it was true and never asked Blaine about it.

Angel signed them in, turning back to her husband.

The love he had for Angel was reflected in his face. There was a time when Blaine had looked at her like that. That morning she'd seen the old him once again.

Turning away from the couple, she gave them their private moment.

"You don't have to stay," Angel said.

"I'm going to stay," Lash said.

"Okay. See you soon." Angel tapped her arm. "Are you ready?"

"Yes."

She nodded at Lash before following behind Angel. They entered a changing room where a couple of women were already standing. Lacey followed in behind them.

"I'm not sure I'm comfortable with this," Lacey said.

"It'll be fun. Please, everyone has a great time here. Give it a moment and you'll enjoy it."

"I've been before, Angel. I'm just nervous. Whizz wanted me out of the clubhouse." Lacey stared at Angel. "Do you know why? It's not about the wedding."

"No. We're here for some fun and relaxation before Christmas truly comes." Angel opened her bag and passed Emily a costume. "We're going to the pool first."

She stared at the black costume Angel handed to her. Emily hadn't been in a costume since she was eighteen years old. That was a long time ago when she didn't have stretch marks.

Taking a deep breath, she smiled at the kind woman then entered a stall.

"Has Lash agreed to another kid yet?" Lacey asked.

"No. He doesn't want to have any more kids. Anthony was a tough pregnancy."

"What are you going to do?"

Emily listened to the women talk. She thought about Angel's responses. They were very quietly answered.

"Do you really want to talk about it?" Angel asked. "I know that you, erm, you can't have any kids."

There was silence for several seconds. Emily was tempted to open the door to watch the two.

"Angel, honey, I can't have kids, but that doesn't mean I can't talk to you about them. Please, do not feel bad or guilty about it."

Emily finished getting dressed. She opened the door to find the two women were hugging. Tears were shining in Lacey's eyes. "I can't have kids," Lacey said, looking toward her.

"I've got one." Emily held her finger up not really knowing what to say.

"Good. I don't want it to be weird between us, Angel. I hope you get pregnant soon." Lacey took a step back.

She felt completely confused. Angel held a towel out to her. "Here you go."

Emily once again followed the two women out of the room. They entered a large area that had several women swimming in the pool. There were a couple of men who wore uniforms and were watching as if they were children.

"There was a woman a year or so ago who jumped into the pool and because we didn't have those guys, she almost drowned. Lash tried to get it changed to women, but that didn't work."

Emily was sure Lash threatened all the men to keep their eyes and thoughts firmly on the job. She walked into the pool, loving the feel of the warm water on her skin.

"I'm just going to swim," Lacey said.

Angel nodded.

Emily walked toward the side of the pool getting used to the water. She glanced across to see one of the lifeguards was watching them or, more importantly, watching Angel.

"So, how is it with Blaine?" Angel asked, completely oblivious to the guy looking at her.

"Erm, we're doing okay." Emily thought about this morning, and her cheeks heated.

"I take it from your color it's going a lot better than okay."

Emily frowned. "Is that why you invited me, to talk about Blaine?" It was Angel's turn to go red. "He told you to bring me here, didn't he?"

"Blaine wanted me to talk to you." Emily made to leave, but Angel grabbed her arm. "Please, don't leave. Blaine's my friend. He trusts me."

She looked down at the water, waiting for Angel to remove her hand.

"He told me what you said to him last night. You don't know if you're in love with him anymore."

"That's my and Blaine's business—"

"I told him that as well. He's worried about you."

Emily didn't know whether to be hurt by how easily Blaine could talk to Angel rather than her, and told her so.

"Blaine loves you, Emily. He confided in me because he's worried."

"He's not the same man I knew."

Angel nodded. "He's changed for you. He stopped the drugs."

She shook her head. "I'm not talking about those changes. The man I met, I was seventeen. It was a bonfire, and he was—I don't know. He was different." Emily stared down at the water remembering the way he'd come up to her as if he had all the confidence in the world. "The man who introduced himself to me, who made me promises, is not the man I see now."

"Do you love Blaine?"

Emily opened her lips then stopped. "I really

don't know."

"What do you think when you think of Blaine?"

"I can't do this, Angel." Emily started to move away.

Angel held her hands up. "I'm sorry. This wasn't my place."

She took off going for a swim. The lifeguard kept looking at Angel. Emily climbed out of the water and decided to warn him.

"The woman you keep staring at is a Skull woman. She belongs to Lash. You keep looking at her like you want her then you're going to find yourself in a world of pain." She brushed past him, wishing someone could say the same about her when it came to Blaine.

Chapter Four

"I'm really sorry, Blaine. I tried to talk to her, but she got really upset. I think you need to talk to her," Angel said, frowning.

Blaine nodded, looking toward Emily as she embraced their daughter. He'd picked Darcy up from her parents. They'd sat down and had a talk. He'd told them of his plan that coming Christmas, and he'd spoken to Whizz. His brother was fine with his plan, providing he didn't spoil things for him when it came to Lacey. From what he heard the meeting with the adoption agency might not have gone so well. Whizz hadn't looked all that great since returning, but the moment he looked at Lacey everything seemed fine.

"Don't worry about it," said Blaine.

"I believe she's still in love with you."

"What?"

He forced himself to stop looking over at Emily to look at Angel.

"Emily's a sweet woman. You can see it, and the only way to remain hurt like that and for this long is because of her feelings for you. Whether she even knows it or not, she's still in love with you, and that's why she's finding it hard to let go. She doesn't want to be hurt again." Angel touched his arm. "I like you, Blaine. I like Emily as well. I'd love to see you both happy."

"Hey, Angel, will you stop touching everyone?" Lash said, coming up to stand behind her. He held Anthony's hand while the boy walked. Lash banded his arm around her waist protectively. "Hands off, Blaine."

Angel slapped Lash's hand. "Stop it. He's got his own problems to worry about." She looked over at Emily who was sitting at the dining room table going through

Darcy's homework.

Emily had bound her hair up on top of her head. The strands cascaded down but exposed her neck. Blaine recalled the times he used to kiss and suck on her delicate flesh. Her neck was one of her most sensitive areas.

"Thank you for all you've done today."

He moved away from the small family to go to his own. Blaine didn't allow Emily's frosty exterior to affect him or send him away.

"Hey, princess, what ya doing?" He leaned down to press a kiss to Darcy's temple while gripping the back of Emily's neck. She didn't jerk away, and he slowly started to caress her.

His daughter looked up at him with those same blue eyes as her mother's. "Math, Daddy. It's hard."

"We'll get it done together."

Blaine stayed standing up, stroking the back of Emily's neck as he helped his daughter to work out all of her problems. When he chanced a glance over at his woman, Emily was staring right back at him, shooting fire with her gaze. He didn't stop. Emily was going to learn that she was his woman and he wasn't going to back down.

Tabitha climbed up on a seat across from them with Eva sitting beside her. "Here you go, honey," Eva said.

"Thanks, Mom."

"What's going on?" Tiny asked, coming to stand with them.

"I'm making Simon a Christmas card," Tabitha said, grinning up at her father. Tate was standing with Simon and her man Murphy, who was currently rubbing her very swollen stomach.

"He's right over there," Tiny said, looking confused.

"Not that Simon."

"Devil's Simon," Eva said.

The look of fury on Tiny's face was clear to see. "I told you to handle this."

"They're friends." Tabitha was oblivious as her parents started to argue over her budding friendship with Devil's little boy.

"I'm not having her thinking she can do this shit, Eva."

"Tiny, they're two friends that have gotten to know each other. In a year they'll both be in fucking school. Back off. It won't be long before they're forgetting each other. Nothing is going to happen between Simon and Tabitha. I promise."

Blaine watched as Tiny nodded.

"For now, just pretend it doesn't bother you. She's young, Tiny. Another guy will come along and be her superhero."

"I'm supposed to be her superhero."

"Then act like it."

Tiny gritted his teeth but took a seat. "Hey, honey, what've you got there?"

"Reindeer, Simon's scared of them, but they're not scary. They're going to help Santa deliver presents."

"Where's his sleigh?" Tiny looked over the paper, but all Blaine could see was a motorbike.

"This Santa is cool like our dads who ride motorbikes." Tabitha grabbed imaginary -handle bars and made brum-brum-brum noises.

Tiny burst out laughing. "God, I love you, sweetheart. You can never change."

"I know, Daddy." Tabitha gave her father a hug.

Blaine finished helping Darcy with her homework with Emily chipping in to help as well. He remembered Emily doing homework when they were together. While she worked he'd sit and watch her, content to just see her.

You fucked up and now you're living with it.

He wouldn't be living with it for much longer. The past was going to finally stay in the past.

"Are we going home now?" Darcy asked, putting her pens away and flipping her homework book closed.

"No, not tonight," Blaine said. "Come on, let's show you to your room." He bent down presenting his back to her. "Get on. You're never too old for a piggy back ride."

"Dad, I'm almost six."

"Complain when you're sixteen."

Darcy giggled and climbed onto his back.

"Tell Mommy to join us," Blaine said. Emily could find any excuse to deny him, but she couldn't tell their daughter no.

"Come on, Mom. Daddy can give you a piggyback ride as well."

Blaine laughed. He'd be more than happy to give Emily a ride or two.

"I'm too big and too heavy."

"No, you're not, Mom."

He decided to take charge. "We are ready for lift off, one, two, three, four ... hold on tight." Blaine started to shake his entire body, loving the giggles coming from Darcy. This was how he imagined life to be when Emily first told him she was pregnant. They would be a happy family with so much love and laughter. He took off, rounding the table and almost colliding with Nash who was doing the same thing to Rachel.

A couple of the brothers shot them glares, clearly not happy with being bombarded with children and all the girl crap that was going on. Blaine didn't mind. He liked the family feel the club always had. This Christmas was more significant than any other. This was about getting back together after Gonzalez had tried to screw them over. They had lost their connection to the Chaos Bleeds crew. Blaine didn't have much interaction with them, but Tiny and Devil had once been firm friends.

Blaine looked forward to Christmas with his women and the club.

He made his way upstairs with Darcy giggling. "Let's go and see where the little angel will be sleeping."

Eva had pulled him aside to let him know she'd made up a room for her, and that it was one where she wouldn't hear anything from the other room. Some of the clubhouse rooms didn't have thick walls to keep the noise out. He heard several of the brothers had complained about the arguments happening between Hardy and Rose. The other kids were sharing a room. Darcy was older than all of the other kids and so she got her own room.

"Mommy, would you please open the door so our princess can see her castle."

Emily stepped forward, turning the handle. Inside was a pink princess palace. Once Eva and the women got their hands on a project, nothing was ever safe from pink.

"Wow, Daddy, this is awesome."

He eased her down, and he watched as she charged toward her bed. She jumped up and down, giggling.

"Mommy and Daddy are going to be next door. You've got to promise me you won't go wandering off without us."

The connecting door was locked. He didn't want to be disturbed at night. Darcy was a good girl, and she'd been sleeping through for a long time.

"I promise." Darcy moved up toward him, wrapping her arms around him. "Will Santa know we're here?"

"Santa already knows it. I talked to him already. We're the best of buds."

"Did you hear that, Mommy?"

"I heard it."

He glanced back to see Emily smiling.

"Can I play?" Darcy asked.

"Sure."

He stood up, taking hold of Emily's hand, and closing the door.

The moment they were alone he saw Emily's fears once again.

"Go ahead, ask anything you want."

****

Blaine had been really sweet. Guilt once again gnawed at her heart to have doubts about his ability to be a father. He'd done nothing but prove how great he was. It was time for her to put all of those doubts to bed. She needed to get over it, as otherwise she was going to live to regret parts of her life.

"Is it safe for her to be alone?"

"We're not pervs, Em. She's safe. All the guys will take care of her."

She shook her head. "No, that's not what I meant. What I meant was the club is known for having a lot of sex. I've seen it myself, Blaine. Will they know the room is in use? She's young."

He reached out and grabbed her arms. She liked his touch way too much. This was what always made her scared. All he needed to do was touch her and she felt herself falling. He was the first and only man she'd ever been with. Blaine was the only man she ever wanted. The very thought of being with anyone else repulsed her.

How could she have doubts about her feelings?

The future terrified her, but being without Blaine

scared her even more.

"Em, Tiny has taken care of it. The brothers are all on board with it. The sweet-butts are on their best behavior. They're not allowed to fuck out in the open. The brothers can still take them but it's in the privacy of their own room. They'll risk being kicked out of the club. When Christmas is over, it'll be different."

She was happier now. Darcy was too young to have sex thrown in her face.

"Come on, this is our room."

Emily had been here a few times with Blaine when the club went into lockdown. All of those times they'd had Darcy in the room with them. This was the first time when they'd be alone without their daughter present. His room was simple, a black carpet, white walls, and several drawer cabinets decorating the walls. There was a wardrobe near a door.

"Does that door lead to Darcy's room?"

"No, this is the bathroom. Tiny hated seeing all the men's asses hanging out, and when he rebuilt the clubhouse, he installed bathrooms into most rooms. There's a shared bathroom around the back, but that's for the sweet-butts. The men have their own rooms and bathrooms. I think he hated the idea of Eva seeing other men's butts."

She laughed, believing him. Tiny was a very possessive man. He wouldn't like the thought of any man getting near his woman.

"About Angel today—"

"Blaine, you really don't—"

"I do. Angel's my friend. She looks out for me, and I trust her with everything. I told her about you and Darcy. I want you to be happy more than anything. From the first moment I saw you, I wanted you. It wasn't just about sex. I love being with you, listening to you talk, watching you think, I love it all. I fucked up today. Please, don't be upset with Angel."

"I couldn't be upset with her. She lives up to her name. She's a sweet woman."

"I've been clean a long time. I got clean after I saw you that last time on your parents' doorstep." She watched as he pulled out his wallet, flipping it open. "You and Darcy kept me going. I'm not going to go back to the drugs or the women. I was an asshole. Words will never be good enough to say how sorry I am. I'm going to prove it to you."

"You're already proving it." She pressed her hand to his chest, directly over his heart. "I'm not going to lie to you. It hurts thinking about you with those other women. I get scared that if I let myself go you're going to back out on your word again." She saw he went to speak and pressed a finger to his lips. "I can't make promises that it's always going to be easy between us. It's not, but I imagine that's the same for a lot of couples. My parents have both asked me to cut you some slack." She laughed thinking about it. "I'm going to try with you. I want to try not just for Darcy but also for us. I think we deserve it as well."

He wrapped his arms around her pulling her close. "I love you, Emily."

She couldn't bring herself to say the words. They had a lot of ground to make up for, but she wasn't going to make it harder anymore.

"I'll move the rest of my clothes into the apartment. You're right, it's time I moved in and gave you more of a chance." She offered him a smile before stepping away.

"You're not going to be disappointed."

"Is it okay if I go and help out with dinner?" she asked. She wanted to go and join the women and try to make herself part of his world.

"Sure."

She stepped back turning toward the door but stopped. Emily walked back to him going to her toes and pressing a kiss to his lips. It wasn't much, but it was the first step.

Leaving the room she walked down toward the kitchen to hear the women talking. Angel, Tate, Kelsey, Eva, and Sophia were all talking about Rose.

"We should invite her," Kelsey said. "She's part of the club."

"She's filed for divorce. Hardy's been a right depressing bastard." This came from Tate in between bites of her candy.

"He loves Rose. He's got a right to be sad," Angel said.

Tate snorted. "He cheated on her. Not only did he cheat on her, he got the bitch knocked up."

Emily stepped into the kitchen.

"Ah, Emily, you'll agree with me."

"I've got nothing to say. I went back to Blaine." He hadn't gotten anyone else pregnant, and she'd not walked in on him actually doing it. She knew Rose and liked the older woman.

"Yeah, but it's different. You didn't change for him, Emily. Blaine has done everything he can to make up for being an ass. What has Hardy done? Nothing. He's taken everything from Rose and given her nothing back. The only reason he hasn't cheated is because Rose made herself available. Blaine had to change in order to get you back. He was high on drugs, and I bet he wouldn't have touched any bitch if he'd been sober. I've seen some of the sweet-butts trying to get his attention, and trust me, Emily, he pushes them away. Blaine's a good boy now." Tate tapped her hand, affectionately.

Out of all of the women, Emily was unsure about Tate. There were times she liked her and then times she wasn't sure she liked her at all. Her feelings confused her about this woman.

"You're talking shit again," Eva said. Tiny's woman had a bowl resting against her waist as she was beating up a mix.

"Stepmom, I'm pregnant." Tate pouted, but Emily saw the glint in her eyes. Tate loved Eva.

"You always talk shit. Has Tabitha talked to you? Don't look all innocent to me, Tate. I know you're close to Tabitha. If you think you can play me, think again."

Tate rolled her eyes. "She's like four years old. Nothing is going on in her little head."

"What about Simon? She talk about him a lot?"

"Yes, she talks about him. I think you should worry when she's a teenager and mooning over him. Really, what is your and Dad's deal about this?"

"He's worried if I don't nip it in the bud it'll flourish into something more."

"There are worse things to happen. Devil's a good father. Even Dad has got to admit that. I've seen him with Simon."

Eva put the bowl down, adding flour to the mix. "I'll guess we'll have to wait and see."

"How is Daisy?" Angel asked.

"She's fine. Her parents aren't much good. Tiny has tried to get him a job, but nothing will take."

Daisy was a young girl Tabitha's age at the nursery where they'd started to take them. Emily had recommended the nursery in town near the church. It was a good place to take kids as Darcy had been there.

"Anthony likes her," Angel said. "Actually, I don't know if he likes her. I've watched the two together. Daisy will sit with a book in her lap telling a story. She's not reading the words, but he listens as if she is." Angel shrugged. "I don't know. It's such a shame as the girl is adorable."

"Can I help?" Emily asked, rolling her sleeves up.

"We've got pastry in the fridge." Sophia pointed to the large fridge.

She walked toward it as the women kept talking amongst themselves.

"Do you think Lacey's got any idea about the honeymoon?" Kelsey asked.

"Nope, and we're to keep it that way."

"What honeymoon?" Emily asked, pulling out the pastry and taking it over to the cool table. She sprinkled flour over the counter and started to roll it out.

"Whizz is making all the preparations to marry Lacey on Christmas Eve. It's going to be so beautiful. When Christmas is over, Whizz is taking her away on a honeymoon. They're going to Spain," Tate told her.

"Do any of you know what's going on with the adoption agency?" Eva asked. "No one has found anything out?"

"No, he's kept quiet about it," Angel said.

"Poor woman. She'll never know what it's like to carry her own child." Eva rubbed her own stomach.

"You got anything to tell us, Eva?"

"Shut up, Tate."

"Rose can't have children either," Sophia said. "It's sad what's going on with her." Sophia was pregnant with her second child as well.

Emily didn't know if she could have another child yet. Darcy wasn't a handful but a blessing. She wouldn't risk the precarious relationship she was in with Blaine. They would have to actually have sex for her to get pregnant again. She thought about that morning and how he'd brought her to orgasm. All he'd needed to do was slide down and he'd have been inside her.

"Are you having any more kids?" Tate asked, looking at her.

Pulling out of her erotic thoughts Emily shook her head. "Not yet."

"Why not? Darcy's an angel. I've seen her, Emily. You've been lucky. Simon can be such a handful. He's taken to throwing shit at the moment."

"Tabitha throws tantrums that give me headaches."

"Rachel's taken up to ignoring me. She'll only listen to Nash."

They all turned to look at Angel. "Don't look at me. Anthony's wonderful. He doesn't cause any problems."

Emily chuckled. "I've seen him. He's an intelligent boy, quiet, but there's something going on there."

"Why don't you want any more kids?" Tate asked. All the women glared at her. "What? You all know I'm nosey. Stop pretending like it's a problem."

"It's okay. There's nothing wrong with you being curious." Emily stared down at the rolled out sheet of pastry. "What am I supposed to be doing?" she asked, laughing.

Angel handed her a round cutter. "We're supposed to be making mince pies. They're Lash's favorite. I made my own mincemeat to go inside."

"Come on, Emily, stop stalling."

She worked from the outer edge and worked her way around to the middle. "I'm not stalling. It's complicated. I was pregnant when Blaine went off the deep end. He started taking drugs, and he became a man I didn't even recognize." She stopped as Angel put the muffin tins down for her to put the pastry inside. "My parents were there for me when I gave birth. I don't want to put any pressure on either of us to have another kid."

"It's not always going to be like that," Tate said. "He really has changed."

Emily shrugged. "I just want to enjoy my time with him without bringing another baby into the mix. The last three years have been pretty hectic. We've not really had the time to, erm, have fun." Thinking over the last three years, she knew the club had been in so much trouble with on enemy or another. For the first time since she'd entered Blaine's life again, it was finally placid.

They all agreed.

"So, Rose," Kelsey said. "She has a right to be here."

"I'll invite her," Eva said. "She's finally getting on her feet. Tiny has told her she's welcome back at the club any time."

"What about Cheryl and Michael with Butch?" Sophia asked. "He's not gone to Vegas yet."

The women went quiet. Butch was still a hard topic.

"They're going to be here," Angel said, speaking up first. They all turned to look at her. "I believe he's going to Vegas with Ned after Christmas. Until then, he's staying at the club with Michael and Cheryl. Alex is going to be there as well. He deserves to see his son around this time of year."

Emily loved Angel's forgiving nature. She understood why Lash got so protective and worried over his woman. The world was not full of good people. There were bad people and there were worse than bad people. There were people out there who'd take advantage of Angel's sweet nature. They'd tear her apart and spit her back out a shadow of herself. Emily truly hoped it never happened. Angel was beautiful to watch and listen to.

All of the women agreed. "It's time we moved on. Gonzalez has taken enough from us. I agree with Angel," Eva said. The other women nodded, and Emily saw them all relax. It was Christmas, and with Whizz getting married, the whole clubhouse together was stressful enough.

"Okay, next order of business," Tate said. "We need to find a date for Baker. I need to see him smile at least once."

Emily laughed as the mischievous group started to make plans involving Baker.

****

Hardy climbed off the back of his bike, throwing the cigarette he'd started into the snow. He stared up at the house he'd shared with Rose for the last ten years. They'd been together longer than thirteen years, but this was the house he bought after all the shit went down ten years ago. The guilt had weighed on his soul in ways he never thought possible. Rose was a beautiful woman back then and now. She'd only grown more beautiful over the years.

He ran fingers through his hair and walked up to the door.

Baker opened the front door. He was the one prospect who looked like he was going to get voted in first. Ink and Fighter were just as good, but they'd not been there when Gonzalez had sent a man to kill Eva. Baker had been there and showed everyone in the club never to underestimate a baker. He was a strong man, and Hardy respected him. Everyone knew he'd lost his family and had nothing left in life other than the club.

"You're not supposed to be here, Hardy. Tiny gave me a call that you'd left the clubhouse." Baker closed the door, standing in front of it.

"Look, I just need to see Rose. I need to talk to

her."

"She asked not to be disturbed."

"Are you fucking her?" Hardy asked, regretting the words once he said them.

"Are you for fucking real? You're going to stand there and accuse me of fucking your woman when I'm here because of you?"

"Shit, I'm sorry." He wasn't used to this. Hardy wasn't used to being jealous of any man. Rose had always treated him like a god. She never put up a fight with him in the past and always gave him what he wanted.

The more she fought him now the more Hardy realized what a shit husband he'd been to her.

"You've got to let it go."

The door opened, and Rose appeared over Baker's shoulder. "It's okay, Baker. I'll talk to him."

"Tiny's rule—"

"I've spoken to Tiny. It's okay."

Baker nodded and left them. Hardy didn't doubt he was watching and he'd be close enough to interfere. Hardy stared at her. Her red hair was pulled back into a ponytail. Hardy had always loved her full red hair. She wore glasses again. Hardy knew it had been a long time since she'd last worn glasses. Was that his fault as well? He recalled asking her to wear contacts, but the glasses made her look sexy as hell.

"What are you doing here, Hardy? Tiny's pissed that you're here. I've told him to let it go. I left without even talking to you."

"I got the divorce papers."

"I only want the house, Hardy."

"This isn't about the fucking house." He couldn't give a shit about the house. Hardy stopped, staring down at the snow covered ground. He was bombarded by all their good memories. The last ten years hadn't been shit. They were good together. He loved her with all of his heart and soul. Hardy knew he couldn't lose her.

He took a step closer but froze as Rose took a step back.

"I'm not going to hurt you."

"I don't want you near me. Stay there or I'm going back inside." Rose held her hand up as if to ward him off.

"Okay, I'll stay here."

"Just sign the divorce papers."

"Why? For ten years we've lived with this. Ten years I've proven I've loved you more than anything else."

"No, you haven't. All you've done is proven to me that if I'm there all the time, you won't stray. I'm the only one who has changed, Hardy. I'm not going to keep changing. Sign the divorce papers. It's time for us both to move on."

She turned back toward the door.

"I'm not going to let you get away from me, Rose. Any man who touches you I'll fucking kill."

Rose turned back to glare at him. Even though he was standing a few feet away from her, he saw the tears in her eyes.

"Even now it's always about you. You're a selfish person, Hardy."

"Don't cry, baby."

"I'll do whatever the hell I like."

The sound of a car approaching had them both looking toward the sound. He saw it was Eva and Emily driving up toward the house.

"What are you doing here, Hardy?" Eva asked, climbing out of the car.

"I'm just leaving." It was pointless for him to

keep trying to get closer to his woman. Rose wasn't ready to talk to him yet. He'd just have to wait until she was.

Chapter Five

"I'm happy for you to get married after me. I'll take Lacey upstairs. I'm not going to be waiting around to party. When I put my ring on her finger that's it for me." Whizz took a sip of his water as he made notes in a book.

"What are you doing?" Blaine asked.

"Tiny wants to invest into the town. He thinks we can open a gym in town. We've not got one, and from what he heard at the town hall, people want one. There's a new health kick going on." Whizz made a few more notes, scribbling shit fast. "I'm looking into the land."

"You know the building that we burnt down is a great location for the gym," Blaine said.

"I know. I'm not sure Lacey's ready for that."

"It's our property now, Whizz. We bought it up. Build it back up and it'll turn over a great profit. It's got a large parking lot."

"It'll bring more employment to the area if we make it great. People will come just to work out," Whizz said, agreeing.

"People come to Fort Wills just to see the fucking club." It was no secret that The Skulls was also an attraction to the town. Blaine didn't know why. There was a lot of danger getting mixed up with the club. They'd all had a lot of deaths to deal with.

"I know. Fighter would make a good instructor, but we'd need him to be voted in before we put him in there." Whizz made another note before slamming the book closed. "Right, I've got everything ready my end for the wedding. Lacey doesn't need any of that fancy shit. I've booked the priest, and I've spoken to him. He'd be happy to join you and Emily together. Lacey's taking care of her stuff with Eva and the women."

"Is there any way you can make Emily's parents present during it? They're, erm, they're going away on a cruise."

"Sure, we can open up a video link. I just need their email and I can get it all set up."

Blaine handed over the email address, hoping Whizz could work his magic. "Thank you for letting me do this."

"Hey, I'm only helping you out. You're the one who has got to get the woman to agree."

"Does Lacey know about the honeymoon?"

"Not yet. She'll know when it's the right time, and I want us both to enjoy Christmas. I've got everything covered here. We'll be voting about this and other shit after this meet."

Tiny opened the office door and called them all in. It was time for church, their group meeting. When he'd been a prospect Blaine hadn't been allowed in the meetings. These meetings were a chance to vote on what the club was doing next.

They all took a seat. Alex was present as well. It had been a couple of weeks since Blaine had seen Alex. The older man had left the clubhouse a couple of months ago and only turned up when there were important matters to discuss.

Lash sat near Tiny with Nash taking the seat next to him. Beside Alex sat Murphy. Down the lines Hardy, Steven, Killer, Whizz, and Zero took their seats. Gash was one of the last men to arrive. Stink, Happy, and a couple of other brothers who'd been on the road took seats.

"What's going on?" Lash asked.

"A couple of our Nomad brothers have requested a position within the club. They want to settle down.

Happy is one of them. Adam and Twisted are another two."

Blaine looked at the man with ink that went up to his neck. He didn't look like the kind of man you wanted to meet on a cold night.

"Does anyone have a problem with them being voted in? They were part of the club over five years ago, but they left to join our Nomad team." Cole Fowler had been part of the Nomad club. He'd not settled for any biker club but was settled down with his own woman, Sandy. It was probably a good thing as having two Sandys in the club would be so confusing. "Nomad" was a select group of men who didn't patch into any one club but had all shown their loyalty to the MC life. They helped out when necessary but stayed on the road. Occasionally some of them would break off from the club and join one of the MCs that had settled in a town or city.

"I don't see a problem. Whizz will run his checks and we'll vote to see the three boys in action," Lash said.

"Good. You can leave now."

Happy, Twisted, and Adam left the room.

"Wait," Nash said. "Why are you called Adam? Is it your real name or road name?"

Adam smiled. "It's a road name and because I'm the one that ends all happiness, mate." His British accent would have the women falling over themselves.

"Stay away from Angel," Lash said, firing out his warning.

"The blonde I've seen, she looks like an angel."

Lash went to get to his feet.

"Sit down, Lash," Tiny said. "I've got rules, and one of those is no poaching other men's women. The sweet-butts can be taken by anyone, but the old ladies are not to be touched."

"I got it. The old ladies don't get to know how good I am."

The three men left.

"I don't like them," Lash said.

The brothers started laughing.

"We've got to give them a chance. I heard Devil is recruiting more men as well."

"This isn't some kind of pissing contest, is it? You want more men because they've got more men."

"No. I've heard the Trojans are also taking on more men. It's something we've all agreed to before."

The Trojans were a club that was well over three hundred miles away. They rarely had anything to do with the other club.

"Okay, let's get down to the next order of business."

"Let's talk about the shit happening to the club," Hardy asked. "I don't like it. This is for the men, not women."

"This is a family club, Hardy. We're all a family. After all the shit that's gone down, we're all coming together for Christmas. Deal with it. I'm not going to be changing shit." Tiny's cell phone went off. "Rose has also agreed to be here. Your life with her may be turning to shit, but she's still part of the club. You better leave her alone. She stopped me today from kicking you to the curb. Anyone else got any issue with what's going on?"

Blaine stayed silent. Christmas at the club meant he got his woman close without losing her.

"Good. It's what I like to hear." Tiny looked down a list he had in front of him. He talked about the town hall and the fair he had planned. "I think if we organize the fair, we can really gather the citizens of Fort Wills to show we're here to stay."

"It'll show we're ready to take responsibility for

what happened," Lash said.

They all knew Lash had to have the majority of input as he was the next in line to take over from Tiny's spot.

"Baker can put his skills to good use," Nash said. "Sophia said he made some kind of éclair or something. She wouldn't stop talking about it. He can bake."

"I'll talk to him," Tiny said. "Now, you all know about Lash taking my place when I'm ready to step down. Do any of you have a reason to complain or want to put in their own vote?"

Silence descended on the room.

"Seriously? None of you want the job?" Lash asked.

"You're good, brother." Nash slapped him on the back.

The last thing Blaine wanted was to run the MC. He loved being a Skull, but the last few years had taught him he was better as muscle than as a leader.

Murphy raised his hand. "I'm not asking for a shot. I want you to talk to Tate. She's not said anything about what's going on. I've not talked to her about it. She'll take it better from you, Tiny."

"I'll talk to her."

The subject of the gym came up. Blaine listened to them dispute the value of building it where they took out the Savage Brothers. Whizz asked for time.

"Lacey's not a Skull," Nash said.

"No, she's my woman, and that makes her a Skull. I'm not saying we not do this. I'm asking for you to give me a couple of weeks. I'll talk to her. We can still go ahead with this project. She won't stop it. I promise."

"Give her time. Talk to her," Tiny said, agreeing. "The next order of business is Butch."

Blaine didn't have a problem with Butch.

"I've got the house set up for the move to Vegas," Alex said. "Cheryl's happy with me spending time with Michael as well."

"Are you sure? We can have Butch stay here if you want?" Tiny asked, but didn't look pleased by his offer. He was obviously only doing it because Alex was his friend.

"I've heard them talking. They're happy for the move to Vegas. Butch wants the chance to prove himself," Whizz said, speaking up.

"We could always beat him to a bloody pulp?" Lash said. "Kidding. Angel's right. I spoke to her about this, and I've got to agree with her. Butch is better off going to Vegas. The only thing I'm interested in knowing is who was working for the Savage Brothers. Even Lacey said Butch tried to lure them away from the town hall."

"Whizz, we're calling on you again."

"You want me to do some digging?"

"You've got the cameras around the town hall and all the footage. Find out who was calling, or I don't know, who had contact with the Savage Brothers prior to all the shit happening."

Whizz pulled out his cell phone. Seconds later he pocketed the device. "Will do."

"We'll keep Butch here and see him off to Vegas with Ned when the season is over. He can be within the club, wear the cut, but he's not sitting in meetings or having any deciding votes."

They all agreed. "Okay, this is our last meeting until after Christmas." Tiny slammed his hand on the table.

Everyone started to get up.

"Oh, if any of you fucking ruin my wedding, I'll hurt every one of you," Whizz said.

They all got up and slapped him on the back.

"Blaine, can I see you?" Tiny asked.

Staying behind, he stood watching the other men leave including Alex. When the door closed, Tiny got up.

"Whizz let me know you're going to marry Emily after he's married Lacey."

"I'm going to try." At the moment he really didn't know if she'd agree or tell him to fuck off.

"Emily's your woman, but claiming her in front of the club is something new. She's not been around the club much so I've never had to pull you aside. There are rules with each woman."

Blaine nodded.

"The Skulls come first. She needs to know she'll be protected, but that also means she keeps her mouth shut about everything. Emily will come under our protection. She'll be provided with a prospect for protection if it's necessary. The club will be open to her."

"It's what I want."

"You need to make sure she knows the women also put the club first. What goes down here remains a secret. Now, you can either talk to her about it or I can ask Eva to talk to her about it."

Blaine held his hand out to Tiny. "I'll sort it, or I'll make sure someone else does." He chuckled. "Cowardly, I know."

"I fucked up with my first wife. Patricia was a sweet woman, but I turned her sour because of this life. I always advise men that they make sure they know what they're doing. This life is a good one. Some women, they don't adapt to it well. To tell you the truth, Angel's surprised me."

Blaine laughed. "Angel's surprised everyone. She's got fire inside her."

Tiny agreed. "I know life's not been easy for you, Blaine. You've come a long way. I'm proud to have you on my team."

He shook Tiny's hand. "Thank you for giving me another chance."

"Get out of here."

****

Tiny watched Blaine leave his office. Seconds later Eva walked in carrying a tray of sugar cookies.

"Woman, you're going to make me fat."

"No, I'm not. I'm going to have you working it off tonight."

"Why?" Tiny asked, staring at his woman with suspicion.

"Baker's taking me to see Lexie. We're swapping gifts."

Tiny groaned.

"I'm not staying over. We're having dinner, and Simon and Tabitha are going to get to wish each other Merry Christmas. Trust me."

He took the tray from her hands, pulling her close to him. Eva's soft body melted against him. Her full tits pressed against his chest. Tiny was an old man, and he couldn't believe she was all his.

"I trust you." He pressed a kiss to her lips. She moaned, wrapping her arms around his neck.

The sound of screaming interrupted the moment. Eva groaned. "I better go and see what's going on."

"Go." He watched her ass as she made her way out of the room. Tiny glanced outside of his office window to see Tate dressed up in a hat, gloves, scarf, and a thick coat. She was pushing Simon on the swing.

He loved his daughter. Tiny loved both of his girls. Tabitha was like Tate in a lot of ways.

Grabbing his jacket he made his way out into the cold.

"Higher, Mommy, higher."

She'd grown so much in the last few years. Murphy was a good man for her. No matter how much she'd grown, Tiny knew the club life wasn't for her.

"Look, there's Grandpa," Tate said, pointing toward him.

Simon kept giggling.

"Hey, Daddy."

He walked up beside her, and he wrapped an arm around her shoulders, dropping a kiss to her temple.

"How are you?"

"I'm fine. I feel like an elephant, but Murphy promised me elephants are cute."

Tiny winced. "I'll kick his ass."

"No need. I already did. He won't be fathering any children soon." Tate blushed, letting him know she'd probably slapped him silly.

"That's my girl." He took over pushing Simon on the swing but kept a hold of his girl. "Tate, I want to talk to you about something."

She looked up at him. "Does this have to do with Lash taking over from you when you're too old and senile?"

He shook his head, laughing. "Yeah."

"Don't worry about it, Dad. I'm not upset by you picking him."

"Why not? The club should have been yours."

"No, it shouldn't. You helped start the club and are its president, but you're not the main owner. All of us have a little part of it. If Miles grows up to be like you or Lash, then yeah, he should get the club, but if Anthony's the one or Simon who show the best leadership then they should get it. I don't want the club, Dad. I only ever wanted Murphy and to be part of your world as well." She pressed a gloved hand to her stomach. "I love being a mother more than anything."

Tears filled Tiny's eyes. His daughter was all grown up. Tiny knew she could be a complete bitch and most of the club members had a love-hate relationship with her, but he adored her. Tate's heart was in the right place.

"Besides, Lash isn't going to kick me out. Angel likes me too much."

She snuggled in close against him.

"I love you, Tate."

"Mom would be proud of you, Dad. Eva's a lucky woman."

He doubted Patricia would be happy, but he liked to think it was true. The club was a good safe haven for them all. He only hoped he could keep it all together and for Lash to handle all shit that came their way.

****

Emily placed the large pot of boiled potatoes in the center of the table. Darcy was walking around the huge table putting knives and forks down for everyone.

"I love it here, Mommy."

She looked over at her daughter and smiled. "I love it, too."

"Can we stay with Daddy all the time?"

"Yes. I'm picking up the rest of our stuff from Grandma and Grandpa tomorrow before they head out on their cruise."

Anthony climbed up into his seat, watching them all work. Angel was cutting the large roast beef while Sophia was putting the roast potatoes onto a platter. Tabitha and Miles were fighting with their knives.

Tate came in with Simon. Her cheeks were rosy as she took a seat at the table. "Dinner smells amazing."

"We all chipped in," Angel said, putting the roast on the table. Vegetables, gravy, and all the other components came to the table.

"Where's Daisy?" Anthony asked as Lash walked into the room. The men started to file in. Blaine came to Emily's side, dropping a kiss to her lips.

"I missed you," he said.

He was melting her again with his words.

"I missed you, too." She stared up at him as heat flooded her pussy.

"Emily, kids are present," Tate said.

"Stop being mean," Murphy warned his wife, taking a seat. He winced as he sat down.

Tate snorted. "That'll teach you to call me an elephant."

"She's got her own parents, Anthony." Angel stroked her boy's head before she began serving. When it looked like he was going to say something more, Lash put his hand on Anthony's hand and shook his head.

Anthony looked disappointed but didn't say anything.

The men walked into the room, and Emily was introduced to three new men. Adam, Twisted, and Happy all took a seat.

"So, Angel, I hear you're a true star in the club," Adam said, his British accent thick as he spoke.

Gash laughed. "Lash will kick your ass."

"Adam!" Tiny growled out a warning.

A sound at the doorway had them all looking up. Rose stood in her coat with Baker behind her. "Eva invited us to dinner."

"Pizza wouldn't deliver, and I was starved," Baker said, taking one of the available seats at the table.

"Baker, near Hardy." Tiny's voice let everyone know they couldn't argue.

Emily saw Hardy's scowl, but he didn't make any comment. She felt sorry for him, but she also liked Rose.

The tension built around the table for several

seconds until finally Adam farted, and everyone turned their anger toward him.

"Sorry, I couldn't hold it."

Rose was the first one to burst out laughing. Within seconds the table erupted into fits of laughter. The kids started blowing raspberries as the food was dished up. Once they started eating, silence fell on the group apart from moans of approval.

When it was over the men stayed behind to do the dishes. Emily took Darcy to her room. They sat watching a movie on her bed. An hour later Blaine joined then, lying behind her. She loved the heat of him behind her. His cock pressed against her ass.

Emily lost the flow of the story as Blaine stroked her hip.

He'd awakened the need inside her that she'd shut down years ago.

With the credits rolling, Emily let Darcy have a bath as she picked a book for Blaine to read.

Darcy came out of the bathroom, dressed in her pajamas.

Emily watched Blaine as he read the story, making the right noises, and she enjoyed it.

Before he finished, Darcy fell asleep.

Together they walked into their own room. Emily's nipples were incredibly tight, and her pussy was soaking wet. When he closed the door, Blaine snagged her wrist and pressed her against the wall next to the door.

He thrust his rock hard cock against her stomach. "Do you feel that, Emily?"

She moaned as he held her hands above her head. He kept hold of both of her hands in one of his as his free hand began to explore her body. His touch left a trail of fire in his wake.

"Are you wet for me, Em?"

"Yes. I need you, Blaine."

"What do you need?"

She whimpered, knowing he was waiting for her to say exactly what she needed.

"Tell me, Emily. I'm not going to do anything until you tell me what you want."

"I want your cock."

"Where do you want it?"

"Inside me."

"Where?"

"Inside my pussy."

They both groaned. He slammed his lips down on hers, sliding his tongue inside. She wanted to hold onto him, but she couldn't as he kept her trapped between the wall and his body.

She was done hiding from what she wanted.

"There hasn't been any other man for me," she said, breaking away from the kiss.

"What?"

"I've not been with anyone. You're the only man I ever wanted."

"Fuck, Emily. I'm so sorry."

She shook her head. "No, it's over, Blaine. I'm done hiding. The person you were is not the person you are now. I want you. I want this."

He released her hands, but he didn't walk away. Blaine sank his fingers into her hair, gripping the length. "I'm sorry for the shit I put you through. I love you, Emily. Always have and always will." He claimed her lips once again with an equal passion to her. She melted against him as his other hand slid across her hip, pulling her away from the wall.

They didn't break apart even as they moved toward the center of the room.

Blaine pulled away first to remove his jacket. She tugged his shirt out of his jeans as he worked the buttons of hers. They fought each other to get them naked. When he went for her jeans, she pulled back to let him. Blaine didn't give her a chance to reach for his jeans. He pushed her to the bed.

She slid back to the center and watched as he removed his jeans. The length of his cock sprang free, and the sight made her mouth water.

He crawled onto the bed. She expected him to settle between her thighs and fuck her. There was no rush to Blaine. He gripped her ankle and dragged her down the bed toward him. The intent in his eyes was clear to see.

"I've been dreaming about this pussy for so damn long. I need to have a taste." She watched him lick his lips before moving closer. He hovered over her mound, staring at her for the longest time.

"What's the matter?"

"You've got a pretty pussy. I like looking at you."

She licked her suddenly dry lips as he simply looked at her without doing anything. There was no doubt about it in her mind. He was torturing her. It wasn't fair.

Emily screamed as he opened the lips of her pussy.

"There she is. There's my pretty little clit."

When they were younger he'd never been much of a talker. He was sure making up for it now. Blaine slid his tongue around the inner lips of her pussy to circle her clit. He didn't touch her clit, taking his time to explore every part of her sex.

"You taste so damn good, and what makes you taste this good is knowing I'm the only man who's been inside you. The only cum you've let inside you is mine.

You're all mine, Em."

She screamed as he sucked her clit into his mouth. The pressure was hard and intense, giving no doubt to his intention.

"Watch me," he said.

Emily went to her elbows to watch him sucking on her clit. She didn't have the energy to be depressed by the sight of her stomach. It wasn't smooth or hard. She had a couple of rolls and the visible sign of stretch marks. Blaine didn't seem to mind. He kept licking and sucking at her pussy.

She couldn't look away as he flicked his tongue across her nub then slid down. Losing sight of his tongue, Emily collapsed to the bed as he fucked her with it. His strokes were solid and wet yet nothing like the feel of his cock inside her. She remembered what it was like to be completely taken over by his dick inside her.

He moved back up to take her nub once again. Blaine was the one in control, and he wasn't giving her a chance to deny him. Emily couldn't turn him away even if she wanted to, which she didn't. The pleasure he was creating was unlike anything she'd ever felt. She'd thought he was amazing when they were both younger. Nothing that he did then could even compare to the expert way he was touching her.

"Please, Blaine," she said, begging.

"What?" he asked, leaving her pussy. "Do you need to come?"

"Yes, please, I need to come." She was desperate for the release that only he could give her with his expert tongue.

"Ask me to make you come."

"Please, Blaine, make me come." She fisted the blanket underneath her, trying to hold onto anything to keep her sanity. It wasn't helping. Nothing was helping as he finger-fucked her pussy then slid the tip of his tongue repeatedly over her clit. The pleasure tore through her body. She reached for a pillow, placing it over her mouth to stop her screams from being heard.

Seconds later the pillow was taken from her. "I can hear those screams. There's no chance of anyone hearing how good you sound when you let go."

She believed him, and when her release finally came, Emily didn't hold anything back. Sinking her fingers into the thick length of his hair, she thrust her pussy up to his face. She needed the release.

He pushed two fingers inside her, fucking her in steady strokes.

Emily came, shaking with the pleasure he'd taken her on. He took her to heaven, but he didn't leave her then for long. She looked up into his dark eyes as he held the length of his cock in his hand and slowly fed his cock into her waiting pussy. It had been too long, and the length of him made her wince.

Five years without sex and she was about to get everything she'd been missing out on.

Chapter Six

Emily's tight hot cunt surrounded his aching dick, and Blaine was in heaven. He'd not been inside such a tight pussy. Blaine slammed the last couple of inches inside her, watching her eyes widen, and a moan escape her lips. She was so fucking beautiful and his, all his. No man had ever tasted her sweet nectar or knew the pleasure that could be had deep inside her body. Emily was fucking perfection to him. He had fucked up in the past, but he wouldn't do it again.

Unlike Hardy, he knew when he had the best person in the world. He would cherish Emily for the rest of his life, and prove to her she was more than enough for him.

"You're so fucking wet for me."

He wasn't wearing a condom, and the feel of her sweet heat surrounding his dick was the best of all.

She gripped his arms with her nails sinking into the flesh.

"Does it hurt?" he asked, seeing the slight pain in her eyes.

"A little."

Blaine stayed still. He didn't want her to remember the pain, only the pleasure. Leaning down, he licked her lips waiting for her to open up so that he could deepen the kiss. Emily responded to him, like all the times before, within seconds. She opened her lips, and he swept inside, plunging his tongue into her mouth.

She moaned, arching up toward him. Her pelvis stayed still, letting him know that she wasn't comfortable with his dick inside her.

He put most of his weight on one hand that he placed beside her head. With his other, he stroked her body moving down to cup the mounds of her tits. They were full, and showed the evidence of her feeding their child together. The sight of her stretch marks didn't repulse him. They turned him on. Emily had given herself to him, and he'd never forget that. He couldn't change the past with them together, but he could change their future and he was determined not to fuck it up again. Emily was his whole world.

Exploring her mouth, he stroked over her nipples, pinching the hard buds between his fingers.

Her groan turned him on, and his cock lengthened further inside her. Breaking away from the kiss, he trailed a path down her neck, sucking on the rapidly beating pulse. Moving down, he claimed one of her nipples. He pushed her breast up so the angle wasn't awkward for him to reach her tit.

She cried out, arching up.

"I can't take much more. Fuck me, Blaine."

He didn't do as she asked. He wouldn't allow her to have doubts or to be sore because he couldn't wait. Flicking the tip of her nipple, he sawed the tight red bud between his teeth, listening to her moan. Her nipples were so sensitive.

Blaine did the same to her other breast, coating the tip in his saliva and then sawing it between his teeth, creating another added element of pain.

"Please, Blaine."

She continued to beg him, but Blaine didn't want to just fuck her. This was their first time. He was determined to make it memorable. Rearing back on the bed, he took a pillow with him, and he slid it underneath her ass, raising her up to meet him. With his cock inside her, he stared down at where they were connected.

There was a dark dusting of pubic hair that covered the lips of her pussy. Running his fingers through the length, he opened her lips to see his cock inside her cunt. It was such a beautiful sight. Her pussy was slick with her cream, which covered his cock.

"I'm going to shave this hair off so when I lick your cunt I can suck all of you inside my mouth."

He stared up into her eyes. Her raven hair was spread out on his pillow, and her gaze was focused on him. She was completely naked, exactly how he wanted her.

"You've gotten dirtier," she said.

"I've aged, baby." He'd aged, and throughout the years of him being alone with only his hand to satisfy him, he'd gotten a shitload of fantasies. Every one of his fantasies featured Emily. He was going to relive each one and take her on a ride of pleasure right alongside him.

Caressing a finger through her slit, he pressed his thumb against her clit. "Are you going to let me?"

"Yes," she said, without hesitation.

He watched her as he teased her clit with his thumb, prolonging her pleasure. With each stroke of his thumb across her clit, her pussy tightened around him. He had to grit his teeth and count sheep in his head to stop himself from fucking her harder than ever before.

Go easy. Take your time.

Blaine eased his cock out of her as he teased her clit. She didn't show any sign of pain, and taking small, shallow thrusts, he began to pump his cock within her.

"Fuck, Blaine. It feels so damn good."

She was gripping the sheet beneath her as he began to fuck her.

"Touch your tits, Emily. Show me what you like."

Her eyes opened, and she stared back at him as she brought her hands to her chest. Blaine saw the hesitation inside her.

"You see this?" He held the fingers he'd been caressing her clit with. The low lighting from the lamps showed them glistening with her cream. "You're soaking wet. When you're with me you don't need to be embarrassed. It's me, Em. Take your pleasure, use me to bring yourself to release." With her eyes on him, he sucked his fingers into his mouth, moaning as he did. The taste of her exploded once again on his tongue. He'd gladly spend the rest of his life licking her sweet, tight pussy.

"Beautiful," he said.

Even though her hands shook a little, Emily began to play with her breasts, stroking her finger over the tight nipples. He didn't look away as she pinched them, causing herself a little pain. Her pussy contracted around his cock getting tighter.

Blaine pressed his thumb to her clit, pulling back the hood to expose her nub. He stroked her clit, watching her come apart within seconds. Her climax had her pulling up from the bed and screaming. He leaned down, taking her lips in a searing kiss as she came.

Removing his hand from her pussy, he gripped her hip as he pressed her back to the bed.

Breaking from the kiss, he stared into her blue eyes. "Are you ready for me to fuck you now?"

She nodded.

Holding up his hand, he waited for her to lock her fingers through with his. When she did, he placed them beside her head, and did the same with the other hand. She was giving as much as he was.

Pulling out of her body until only the tip of his cock was inside her, Blaine waited, watching the anticipation grow in her eyes.

In one thrust he slammed back inside her. She cried out, wrapping her legs around his waist. For several thrusts, he made her wait between each one. Only when she begged did he give her what she wanted.

He wouldn't last long, and he claimed her lips as he rammed inside her, over and over again. Blaine fucked her hard, filling every inch of her pussy. She met his thrusts, lifting up to meet his strokes. He wanted to get so deep inside her that she'd forget every shit thing he did, and only remember this moment.

"I love you, Emily. I always have, and I always will."

She didn't say anything to him. Emily hadn't told him how she felt, only her doubts. He'd change that. By the time Christmas came he was determined she would have no doubts when it came to him. She shouldn't have doubts, and it was his fault that she did.

Being years without her pussy, Blaine couldn't control himself, and with a few thrusts, he erupted inside her. His cum filled her pussy as he held her tighter. She hadn't come a third time, but at least he'd brought her to orgasm twice before he found his own.

The blood pounded through his veins as he filled her. Grunting out his release, he collapsed over her. He covered her with his body weight, surrounding her.

Emily stroked his back as he tried to regain his sense of equilibrium. She'd fucked him. All of his senses were askew.

"Blaine, you're crushing me."

He stayed inside her body and moved off her slightly to stare down at her. She stared at him, caressing the tips of her fingers down his arm.

"You're not having any regrets?" he asked.

She shook her head. "No regrets."

Guilt filled him as he'd taken her without a condom. He'd not wanted anything to be between them. "I, erm, I didn't use a condom."

"It's okay. I'm on the pill."

"Why?" Jealousy hit him. She said she'd not been with a man. Had she lied?

"I've never been regular. You know, for my monthly cycles." Her cheeks were bright red as she talked.

He felt like a jerk for being jealous.

"The pill helps to regulate my cycle. It's why I didn't stop you when you didn't reach for a condom."

"What about if I was safe?"

"I decided to put my trust in you. I doubted you'd hurt me. You've told me enough times that you don't want to hurt me. I figured I'd believe you."

"Thank you, Emily."

"I'm not ready to have more children, Blaine. We've got a long way to go to get to having children."

He traced a path around her nipple dipping down to her belly button. "I'm going to make sure we get that chance."

She smiled up at him. "I know you are."

"You're not going to fight me anymore."

Emily shook her head. "No. I'm tired of fighting you. I'm getting the rest of mine and Darcy's clothes tomorrow before my parents leave for vacation. Can you believe they're going on a cruise for Christmas?"

Blaine laughed. "I don't know if we should be talking about your parents with my dick inside you. It's kind of creepy."

She burst out laughing. He loved the sounds she made.

"No, it's a little creepy, I agree." She rested her hands behind her head. This was the most fun they'd had for a long time. "Where did you go after, erm, after you came to see me five years ago?"

He returned his gaze to hers. "You've never

asked before."

"I tried to convince myself I didn't want to know. I do. I want to know what happened. It's time for me to know."

"I left your place holding the photo." He decided to leave out the thought process he'd fought off trying to convince himself that Darcy wasn't his. It had been a stupid thought back then, and an even bigger one now. "I ended up at the bus stop not far from where you live. Lash came to see me. He started talking about being the bigger man and about how when he found the woman for him, he'd not stray." Blaine wouldn't go into the depth of their conversation in the past. The last thing he wanted Emily to be reminded of was his stupid, crazy assed actions. "He told me the best thing for me to do for you, Darcy, and the club was to get clean. He handed me a leaflet for a rehabilitation center. It changed my world, opened up my mind, and made me realize I'd been living a lie. The drugs, they completely changed who I was. I learned the effects of the drugs screwed with my mind." He laughed, thinking about how he finally got sober and clean only to remember what he'd done to his woman. "I couldn't get away from what I'd done to you. It was like I suddenly woke up from a bad dream, but I'd been living the dream. I lost you."

Emily was crying as she looked at him.

"Don't cry for me, baby. I was a fucking idiot. I deserved everything I've been through."

*****

Emily finally saw the true pain he'd been going through. Whenever he'd tried to talk to her about the past she'd cut him off as the memories were too hurtful. She couldn't handle the pain knowing what he'd done.

Tears glistened in his own eyes, but they didn't fall.

"These tears are not needed." He wiped underneath her eyes, rubbing them away.

They had lost so much time.

"I'm sorry."

"No, you don't get to be sorry," he said. "You had nothing to be sorry for. All you've ever done in your whole life is be honest and caring. I fucked up. This is all on me. It wasn't because you were pregnant. I don't know why I took the drugs or why I did what I did. I only know that you're never going to see that side of me again. No matter how tough life becomes, or dangerous, I'll be here, being the man you can count on." He pressed his palm to her stomach. "I missed the birth of my little girl because of my habit. I'm not going to miss another moment of my life with you. You're it for me, Emily. The woman I love."

He was making her fall in love with him all over again. She reached up to touch his cheek. "I thought I lost you."

Blaine took hold of her hand, pressing a kiss to the inside of her wrist. "You could never lose me. When I went to that bonfire all those years ago, you were the only woman who held my attention. You're the only woman I've ever wanted." His cock began to thicken inside her as he spoke. "I'm not going to lose you again. I'd die for you."

She laughed. "I don't need you to die. I need a shower though. I smell. It has been a long day." Emily pressed a kiss to his hard lips, giggling as he collapsed beside her.

"I don't have the energy to move."

"You have the energy. You're so going to have a wash before we get back into the bed."

He eased out of her, slowly. She groaned as his cum spilled from her pussy. Blaine didn't move away.

His gaze was between her legs.

"Now that's a sight I love to see."

"What?"

"You, dripping with my cum. Best fucking thing ever." He climbed off the bed, and before she could move to follow, he swept her up in his arms.

"Blaine, what are you doing? This is insane. I can walk."

"I don't know what you're trying to say. Are you calling me a wimp?"

"No, I'm telling you that I'm heavy. You're going to pull your back out or something."

"I'm not going to drop you." He held her tightly to his chest even as she fought him. In no time he had her dumped in the shower and turned on the water. She cried out as cold water blasted her. Blaine climbed in behind her.

"I'm going to get you for that," she said, growling as he locked her near the cold water.

It was official. Blaine was evil. The water heated up in no time, but she wasn't impressed as he started to laugh.

"Now, you said I could shave your pussy lips." He pressed her up near the far wall away from the cascading water. "And good news for you, baby, I've got a new razor designed for the job."

She rolled her eyes as she started to see her old man back. Blaine would tease her all the time, not in a malicious way, just in his own loving way. She did believe him when he said he loved her. Emily just couldn't bring herself to admit the truth to him. She was scared of what would happen. They were getting along, and she didn't want to ruin that stab of happiness they'd obtained together in such a short time.

Blaine knelt on the floor of the shower lifting one

of her legs up. He held a bar of soap. She watched as he worked the lather into his hands before going between her thighs.

Closing her eyes, she bit into her lip to try to contain the pleasured groan his touch always inspired inside her.

When his hands left her body she looked down to see her hair was lathered in soap. He lifted one knee and placed her foot onto his knee. "Don't move. I don't want to cut you."

"Do you think I should do this?"

"No. You'll stand still so I can get your pussy nice and shaven."

She was awkward with the way she was standing. Emily watched as he slid the razor across the lips of her sex. Some water had pooled in the bottom of the shower. There was enough for him to clean the razor before going back to her pussy. She stayed still doing exactly as he asked while he worked his magic over her pussy.

Minutes passed with him taking his time to get a clean shave. When it was done, he used his hands to wipe away the excess soap.

"Now, that is a pussy to taste."

She didn't get far as he opened her legs and latched onto her clit.

Emily cried out at the instant pulse of heat between her thighs.

He didn't keep up with his touch. Blaine pulled away getting to his feet. "That'll be perfect for me." He banded an arm around her waist, dragging her closer to the spray of water.

She opened her mouth to protest only to find his lips on hers once again. Emily wrapped her arms around his neck, holding on tight to him as he gripped her hips, working down to cup her ass. Emily froze as one of his hands went between the cheeks of her ass to tease the puckered hole of her anus.

Pulling away, she looked at him. She'd read about anal sex, of course she had. Her mother had left some dirty books in her room to read. Emily couldn't believe how open her mother could be at times. Fortunately, Shirley wasn't into keeping everything in the dark. The books provided had been ménage, BDSM, and biker books. There was so much she had to learn.

Anyone would find it strange for a parent to provide sex books, but her mother wasn't normal. She considered reading the same books an act of bonding.

Pushing thoughts of her mother out of her mind she focused on Blaine's lips as he stroked her ass.

"I'm going to take you here soon, Emily." He tilted his head to the side. "You don't seem shocked."

"You'd be surprised why."

"Tell me."

Nibbling on her lip, Emily told him the truth to which Blaine burst out laughing. "You've got some strange parents. They're awesome though. Most kids would love to have them growing up."

Her mother wouldn't have dreamed of giving her sex books when she was growing up. Emily wasn't under any illusions that the only reason Shirley gave them to her was because she was well over the age of consent, and had a daughter of her own.

One of his hands moved around to the front of her body. She gasped as his finger slid through the lips of her pussy going down to finger her cunt.

"Blaine?"

"Don't be afraid with me, Emily. I've had a lot of time to think about us together. A lot of time and a lot of yearning to have you in my life. I've got a lot of fantasies I want you to live out with me."

"What if I don't match up to your fantasies?"

He pumped his finger inside her several times. "You feel how wet you are?" She nodded. "This is one of my fantasies, and you're making it better than even I imagined it and it was all inside my head."

She giggled, resting her head onto his shoulder as he touched her ass and pussy. The water cascaded down them. She opened her eyes to see his cock standing out rock hard and proud. Reaching between them, she grabbed his cock.

"Fuck, baby," he said.

Glancing up, she saw it wasn't pain that had him cursing but pleasure.

Working his cock up and down, she teased the slit at the tip that was leaking out pre-cum.

"You've got no idea what your touch does to me. I feel alive when your hands are on my body."

"You're alive anyway."

"No, not like this." She saw he was serious and didn't mock him. When Blaine touched her, the rest of the world fell away so only the two of them existed.

He pressed his thumb to her clit, working her body to orgasm. She wanted him to come with her. Emily didn't let up from working his cock.

"You keep that up and I'm going to come," he said.

She smiled. "That's what I want."

He growled but added a third finger inside her, thrusting harder inside.

Emily cried out as with a final caress of his thumb she splintered apart in his arms. Blaine followed her. His seed spurted out of the tip to coat her stomach. They were both gasping for breath as Blaine took her lips. This was the start of their new life, and Emily was going to stop looking at the past and only pay attention to the future. She was tired of wanting him but holding herself back. Emily wasn't doing this for Darcy. She was doing this for herself. If she didn't then she'd only live her life with regrets.

****

Baker relaxed sipping his beer as he watched the football match playing on the television. All the tables and stiff backed chairs had been changed for leather seats so that the main bar was more like a sitting room than a bar. No one would believe this room was the place the sweet-butts worked their magic and got fucked.

Fighter had taken Rose back home after dinner, so it was Baker's time off. Tiny had already spoken to him about the bake-off for Christmas, and he wasn't sure if he wanted to do it. He'd not cooked for a crowd since his wife and kid had been killed.

Adam, one of the guys being given a chance to join the Skulls, sat down with him. The other man had been a biker for a long time. He'd been a Nomad, a guy who travelled from place to place without settling for one club or one town.

"The tree's fucking ace," Adam said, with his strong British accent.

"The old ladies know what they're doing."

"That they do. Is Lash always like, you know…"

"Protective, deadly, threatening bodily harm?" Baker asked. Adam nodded. "Yeah, pretty much. No one touches or harms his woman. Angel's to be protected at all costs."

"I heard the rumors but didn't know it was possible. I knew Lash as a small lad. Wouldn't put him down as the ball and chain one."

"I wouldn't say shit to him. Lash doesn't look at other pussy, but no one talks smack to Angel." Baker took a sip of his beer as the bell rang on the door.

Both men froze and looked at each other.

"Who the fuck would ring the bell?" Adam asked.

Getting to his feet, Baker pulled his gun out of the back of his jeans, removed the safety, and moved toward the door. "Who is it?" he asked, shouting the words through the door.

"It's Millie Levy. I've got the toy delivery Eva asked me to bring."

"I'll go and check," Adam said, getting to his feet.

Putting the safety back on his gun, and putting it back in his pocket, Baker opened the door.

A wave of cold blasted at him, but it was nothing compared to the kick in the gut he got when he caught sight of the supposed Millie. She smiled up at him. "Hi, I've not gotten it wrong, have I?" She held a card in her hand. "Eva said to drop it off at the clubhouse and not her home." Millie lifted the card for him to see. Her gloved hands stopped him from seeing if she was taken or not. All thought left him as he stared into her kind face and warm eyes.

She kept staring at him. "Erm, have I got the wrong place?"

"No, you haven't," Eva said, rushing out. Baker glanced back at Tiny's woman to see she was disheveled. It didn't take a lot of guesses to know what they had been up to.

Millie smiled over at Eva. "I've got the car full like you asked." She took a step back going into the cold once again. Her thick coat hid the curves from view.

"Tiny, come on. Help," Eva said.

"I'm coming, woman." Tiny and Adam came out of the room. "You keep farting, Adam, and I swear you're going to find another club."

"What? It got you out of the room."

Baker walked out toward the car, not interested in listening to Adam give some kind of excuse.

The trunk of her car was up, and Mille was pulling out large sacks of gifts. He stepped up behind her, and as she straightened he got a strong scent of vanilla.

She turned around. "Eva ordered quite a bit of stuff."

"I can see that."

Millie's smile disappeared. "Erm, it shouldn't take long unloading the car." She brushed past him to enter the clubhouse.

Eva came out along with Tiny and Adam. They all took two trips each to empty out the car. Millie put the last bag down on the floor turning toward Eva. "There. Your order is complete." She pulled out a sheet of paper. "Please let me know if there are any problems."

"Will do, Millie. You're a star. Do you want to stay behind? I've got hot chocolate on the go."

Baker stared at her hoping she'd stay and hoping she'd go.

"No, it's okay. I'm on a diet. Could you let Blaine know that his order came in? He'll know what I mean."

"Sure."

She left the clubhouse. Going to the door, Baker watched her leave, hating the feelings twisting in his gut.

Chapter Seven

Blaine opened his eyes to find Emily asleep beside him. Glancing over at the clock he saw it wasn't even seven yet. He wiped the sleep from his eyes as he looked over at his woman. She looked so peaceful in sleep. Emily lay on her front with both of her arms underneath her pillow. The blanket had ridden down her body exposing the naked length of her back. His cock hardened as the globes of her ass were visible to his view.

Pulling the hair off her shoulder, he laid a kiss to her exposed flesh before sliding down to press another bunch of kisses down her back until her reached the globe of her ass.

"What are you doing?" she asked.

Her voice was dreary from sleep.

"I'm making you feel good. Lay back and enjoy it." He rolled her over so that she was on her back. Running his hands up the side of her body, he cupped her full tits, pushing them together. He stroked her nipples, pinching them into hard points.

Blaine moved down until he was directly over her naked pussy. Opening her lips he latched onto her clit, sucking her into his mouth, moaning as the taste of her exploded on his tongue.

She groaned, arching up, and thrusting her pelvis against his face. Emily sank her fingers into his hair, holding onto the length as he worked two fingers into her cunt. She was wet already. He teased her nub, focused on making her come. She cried out his name, her pussy tightening around his fingers as she hurtled into a mind-shattering orgasm.

He flipped her back onto her stomach, lifting her

up to her knees. Gripping his cock, he aligned the tip to her entrance, and slid deep into her cunt.

Their moans mingled on the air as he worked every inch of his dick inside her. He gripped her hips, staring down at where they were connected. Blaine saw her puckered ass, which was calling to him to be filled. He licked his thumb, getting it nice and wet before he pressed it against her ass.

She groaned, pushing back against him. Her wanton behavior encouraged him to press a little bit harder to her ass. With his other hand, he held her in place as he began to fuck her hard, taking her in smooth strokes that went deep into her pussy.

"Yes, fuck me, Blaine. Harder."

He gave it to her harder and pushed his thumb past that tight ring of muscles, going into her ass. She cried out, but he didn't go any further. He stilled within her. Blaine wouldn't hurt her. Touching and teasing her ass was about getting her used to feeling him there.

Blaine pounded her pussy.

The sight of her taking his cock and thumb was too much for him. He grunted as he filled her pussy once again with his cum.

He held onto her hips tightly. When he was finished, he pulled out of her body, and walked into the bathroom. Blaine grabbed a towel, washed his hands before he went back to Emily. She was still on her knees, and she was watching him as he appeared in the bedroom. Her blue eyes were cautious as she looked back at him.

Blaine cleaned her pussy before taking a seat beside her.

"What's going on in that head of yours?" he asked.

"I liked what you did with your thumb."

"Why do you look worried?"

"Should I have liked it so much?" She rolled over, sitting up. Emily covered her body with the blanket, and he mourned the loss of the view of her beautiful body exposed to his gaze.

He reached out and pushed more hair that had fallen over her shoulder out of the way. "There's nothing wrong with you liking it so much. I like touching you and bringing you pleasure."

She ran fingers through her hair. The just fucked look suited her. His cock stirred once again.

"I've got to get Darcy ready for school. It'll be over soon. I've also got to gather the rest of our belongings from my parents."

Emily started to get out of bed, but he stopped her with a hand on hers. "Don't hide from what you want. If you want me to fuck you until you're raw, I will. There's nothing we can't do together."

She nodded. "It just takes some getting used to." Emily took the blanket with her. He watched her walk around the room then stop to look back at him. "I've had to put all of *those* needs aside while I raised Darcy. I don't need you to apologize. I'm just asking you to give me time to be comfortable enough to explore it."

He stood, completely naked, letting her see the evidence of what she did to him every time he was around her. "This," he said, gripping his cock, "is all yours. This is what you do to me. You don't have to hide behind a blanket, Emily. You turn me on just by being you."

He saw the indecision in her eyes. A small victory was won as the blanket went to the floor between them.

"I'll get dressed."

Blaine sat on the bed and watched her move

around his room. This was another fantasy of his, and he was going to enjoy the first morning of many to come.

****

Emily waved to her daughter with Blaine standing beside her. They were both wrapped up in jackets, scarves, and gloves as the snow had fallen thickly. The roads were still clear, but Blaine wouldn't be riding his bike for some time. Several of the moms were watching Blaine as they saw their daughter off to school. One of Blaine's arms was over her shoulder, pulling her tightly against him.

"It's fucking freezing."

"I heard Angel was putting on a chili for tonight."

"I doubt it'll make much difference."

They made their way over to the car, climbing inside. Blaine was the one driving. This was the first time they'd be together to go and see her parents. She didn't know if she could look her mother in the eye after what they'd done that morning. Blaine didn't seem worried as he drove toward her parents' house. It was still early in the morning as Darcy needed to be in school by nine.

"You've always hated the cold," Emily said, staring out of the window at the passing scenery. Fort Wills always looked so beautiful in the winter, especially Christmas. The town had splurged out on new decorations. The church was also aglow for the season. She, for one, loved the festive season and looked forward to celebrating this time of year for the first time as a family.

The Skulls clubhouse was constantly alive with activity, and a moment didn't go by when something wasn't going on. She loved the way the women converged on the kitchen to bake and cook. It wasn't just the kitchen though. It was throughout the whole clubhouse. She walked into the games room to find Zero and Prue teaching Anthony and Miles how to play pool on a child's pool table. They were all a family. They were a biker club that cared about one another. There was no crap taken by the outside world. The club took care of one another. They partied and played hard, but they loved even harder. Tiny was a caring man.

"What are you thinking about?" Blaine asked.

"I'm thinking about the club."

"What about it?"

"I've heard the gossip around Fort Wills for years. There're so many rumors about the place, but none of it is true. You're a family."

Blaine chuckled. "Don't be completely fooled. We're a family and loyalty's the key, but a lot of crap has gone down in the club. Tiny demands the best of all the men."

"I get that." She hadn't been oblivious to the stuff that went down. Blaine tried to keep most of the stuff close to him, but she'd known it affected him. He was always trying to protect her.

"I'm sorry. I'm so used to people saying shit about the club."

"I've not got a problem with the club. I know you love it and the life."

"It has always been about you, Emily. The club it offered me a home. I was one of the oldest prospects the club ever had."

He'd turned his life around, and all she'd done was making it harder for him. Glancing down at her hands, she tried to think of the right words to say to him. She didn't want to tell him that she loved him. It was too early for that. Emily didn't know what she was waiting for. She had stopped fighting him because she didn't want to hide anymore from her feelings. She did love him and was tired of always being miserable. There was a time when she had loved without fear. It had been too long since she'd allowed herself to relax. Giving birth, being a mother, the responsibility at such a young age had forced her to grow up. Now Blaine had showed her at every opportunity that he wasn't going to fuck it up. It was time for her to stop fighting and to give him the trust he'd earned.

"You got shot for the club."

"I protected the club women. I wouldn't change what I did, Emily. If I hadn't taken that bullet for Angel I wouldn't have gotten to see you."

"You don't know that."

"Angel came to you, baby. She brought you back into my life. I'll always be grateful to her for that."

She winced as she thought about the times he'd been injured. Blaine hadn't been lucky the past couple of years. She'd sat beside his bed as he'd been recovering. The fear of never talking to him had left her so heartbroken. The only person who'd made these last three years unbearable was her. She had a lot to make up for.

No more. She wouldn't allow her own pain to interfere in their future.

Blaine pulled up outside of her parents' house minutes later. They didn't live far from the school, but he'd taken his time. She didn't blame him. The roads may be cleared, but if ice had set they were screwed. She climbed out of the car and walked up to the front door.

"Do they know we're coming?"

"They should know. I did tell them we're coming." She knocked on the front door, waiting for them to answer.

Emily heard a little squeal and then her mother opened the door. Shirley's hair was mussed, and her cheeks were red.

"Honey, what are you doing here?"

She saw her mother's shirt buttons were mismatched. "Seriously, I don't want to know what you were doing," she said.

Shirley closed her mouth as she'd opened it to explain or lie. Emily was so embarrassed. Her mother was more open about her sex life than she was. Blaine was chuckling behind her.

"Hi, Shirley."

"Shit, you're here for the rest of your stuff. I did remember. I put some eggy bread in the oven to bake." Emily's stomach chose that moment to growl. "See, I'm not a bad mother."

Her father came to the door behind her mother.

"Blaine, it's good to see you," Lenard said.

Going inside the warm house, Emily removed her jacket, gloves, and scarf while Blaine did the same. Her father took him into the sitting room while she followed her mother down to the kitchen. The oven was indeed glowing with the evidence of her cooking.

"You're looking better I see," Shirley said. "Darcy in school?"

"Yes."

"How's she taking your move back with Blaine?"

"She's happy. I did talk to her about it before I decided to do it."

"It's time you gave him a chance."

Emily took a seat at the kitchen counter as her mother filled the kettle. "Are you looking forward to your cruise?"

"Yes. I'm sorry we're not going to be here for Christmas. We really thought it would do you good to have the season with Blaine. He deserves it."

She didn't argue. Emily was really looking forward to spending the season with him and with the whole of The Skulls.

****

"Do you have everything you need for the big day?" Lenard asked.

Blaine glanced behind him toward the door. "I've got to pick up the rings. Millie, the woman who owns the toy shop, got them for me."

"When are you going to get them?"

"After I've taken her back to the apartment. Whizz is giving me a call so I've got an excuse to leave her. I'll pick the rings up, then Darcy, and then Emily before making our way back to the clubhouse."

Lenard nodded. "I'm proud of you, son. I didn't put my faith in you for you to let me down and you haven't."

"I don't know if she'll agree to marry me yet. I hurt her a lot."

"She'll agree, and she'll marry you."

"How do you know?" Blaine asked, truly curious to know.

"I see the way she looks at you. She loves you, Blaine, and she'll marry you."

He really hoped her father was right. "It means a lot to me that I've got your blessing."

"Speaking of blessing, this is for you."

Blaine took what he was offering. He saw a simple diamond engagement ring. "I'm picking a ring up today."

"You're picking a wedding ring up. That is an engagement ring. Shirley wanted me to give it to you to put on Emily's finger before the wedding band. Shirley's mother gave it to her to give to Emily. When Emily was a little girl she'd sit for hours playing with the ring on her grandmother's finger. It was promised to Emily in the will."

Blaine closed his hand around the ring, determined to protect it with his life.

"Thank you."

"Don't mention it. All I need is for you to promise me that you'll love my little girl for the rest of her life."

"I promise," Blaine said, meaning every single word.

****

Eva pulled up outside of the diner. Tabitha and Miles were getting restless for the toilet. Ink climbed out of the car and helped her take the two kids inside along with the gifts she'd bought for Lexie. The other woman wasn't alone as Spider was sitting in a booth several tables down.

Tabitha and Miles charged for the toilet, and Eva followed them. Ink placed the gifts on the table beside Lexie without saying a word.

Eva relieved herself as the twins washed their hands. She washed her hands, drying them quickly as her kids were already out of the room.

Walking toward Lexie she saw Tabitha hugging Simon tightly. Nibbling her lip, Eva slid into the booth.

"Tiny's not happy about that," Eva said, nodding toward their kids embracing. They were sitting together, handing each a card.

"Devil isn't either. He didn't want me to come today, and he almost had a fit at Simon for making her a card."

"I'll be fine. I'm sure it'll be fine," Eva said.

They sat watching Simon and Tabitha. Eva's gut tightened. The only person Tabitha had gotten close to was Daisy, but even her friendship with the other girl wasn't anything like this.

"I can't bring myself to pull them apart," Lexie

said.

"You don't know, they may be the two to bring the clubs back together.

Lexie snorted. "It would have to be. Devil wants nothing to do with The Skulls."

"Same here." Eva reached across the table to grip Lexie's hand. "How are you?"

"We're all good. Gonzalez is gone. We're having Christmas at the clubhouse. What about you?"

"Tiny's preparing Lash to be president." She didn't talk about the other details of the club. Lexie was her friend. "I'm pregnant," Eva said.

Lexie squealed, getting up to hug her. "How far along?"

"Not far but I've not told Tiny. I don't want him to worry. He's got a lot on his mind right now." She turned to look at Tabitha. Her daughter was going to grow into a beautiful girl. Just looking at Simon, she knew he was going to be as badass as his father. This was going to be a disaster.

"Eva, stop worrying. They're going to grow up, and it'll be different."

"I'm just scared she'll fall for Simon and he'll be gone from her life."

"Hey, don't worry. I'm a good mother, and I'm teaching him all the awesome things he needs to know."

Eva laughed. She wouldn't worry until it was absolutely necessary. Staring at their kids she saw Simon held Tabitha's hand tightly as they colored in a book. Lexie may think they were going to grow out of it, but Eva knew differently. Simon and Tabitha's lives were intertwined, and there was no stopping it. Eva only hoped her daughter wasn't hurt too badly when everything went down.

Chapter Eight

It hadn't taken him long to get the ring, and he'd decided to drive back to Emily rather than wait in the cold for Darcy. He had enough time to have some fun with his woman before they got their daughter.

Entering his apartment building, he made his way upstairs thinking about his woman waiting for him. He pulled out his key and walked into the apartment.

"Baby, I'm home. Whizz just needed something from town." He closed the door, walking down the long corridor to the kitchen. Blaine froze when he saw a fake blonde with big tits and too much makeup sitting on his sofa.

"Hello, Blaine."

"Where the fuck is Emily?" he asked, looking into the kitchen.

"She's around my house. I couldn't change the light bulb, and she offered to do it for me. I came here looking for you to change it for me." She got to her feet, and he saw she wore a dress that only just covered her ass.

"What?" Blaine was confused. Why the fuck was Emily around this woman's apartment and not her?

"Don't worry, baby, I was waiting for you."

Okay, he was even more confused. "Who the fuck are you?"

"Don't you remember me?"

"No."

"My name's Nicole. We spoke when you first moved in."

"Fuck this." He turned toward the door ready to go and get his woman.

"Wait."

Before Blaine could stop the woman, she grabbed him, pressing him up against the wall with surprising force. Her lips were on his and he was fighting her off him when Emily chose that moment to walk into the apartment.

"I changed it, Nicole." Emily froze with a set of ladders under her arm. "What the fuck are you doing?"

"I'm so sorry, Emily. I can explain."

Emily looked toward him with a raised brow. "Get the fuck out of my apartment. That's my man, and from the look of horror on his face, you tried to attack him."

"I didn't."

"Get out," Emily said. She dropped the ladders, charging down the corridor. Blaine got turned on as he watched his woman grab Nicole's hair and drag her out. "Get your skanky ass out." She threw the woman out of the apartment.

"Okay, I'm now turned on."

Emily walked up to him, and she used the sleeve of her shirt to wipe his lips. "I'm not kissing you with skank on you." Her lips were on his seconds later. Blaine wrapped his arms around her body, holding her tightly.

"You've got to tell me what the hell just happened. I came home expecting you, not to see her."

She groaned, dropping her head to his chest. "I was an idiot. She came around needing a light bulb. I had a spare and then she needed ladders. I told her to stay here in case you came back and worried. I must have left the apartment as you came around the corner. I was gone five minutes tops. I should have known she was trying to get to you. She's been trying to get to you for a long time."

Disgusted at the thought, he sank his hands into her hair. "She repulses me, Emily. I can't stand her."

"I knew she wanted you, but I didn't expect to be gone so long. I left her here just in case." Emily pressed a hand to her head. "I'm so stupid at times."

"You're not stupid." He pressed a kiss to her lips. "However, you can make it up to me for coming home to her here instead of you."

Running his hand from her neck down to her tits, he stroked her nipples with his thumb."

"I've got a fantasy," she said.

His cock went from flaccid to rock hard in seconds. "Tell me about this fantasy."

"How about I show you?"

She took hold of his hand leading him toward the sofa. All thought of Nicole left his mind as she pressed him to the sofa. Staring up at his woman, he watched as her hands went to the button of her shirt. She pushed the shirt off her shoulders before going to her jeans.

His mouth went dry as she wriggled her hot body out of the jeans. She was curvy, and though some men might not like her rounded curves, he loved them. They were so hot, and he wanted her more than any woman.

"Take your pants off," she said.

Getting to his feet, he kicked off his boots, feeling like a kid getting his first taste of sex. Sitting back down, his cock pressed against his boxer briefs. The only reason he wore the briefs was for an extra layer of protection against the cold. During the summer he didn't bother with underwear, preferring to hang free. She wore a sexy red lace bra with a matching pair of lace panties.

"Show me that pussy of mine," he said.

"This is my fantasy, which means you get to be quiet."

Closing his lips, he watched as she straddled his lap. There was a nervousness to her actions, showing him she wasn't as confident as she made out she was.

Cupping her hips, she rubbed his cock against her covered mound. "Do you feel that, baby? That's what you're doing to me. It's only you and me here, and you've got no reason to be embarrassed."

She gripped his shoulders tightly. "Are you sure?"

"We're in this together. No fear, no regrets."

Emily nodded, biting her lip.

He reached down to grab her ass. "Show me your fantasy. I'll try to live it out for you."

Her hands moved from his shoulders to cup his face. He tilted his head back, giving her free access to his mouth. Blaine squeezed the globes of her ass in his palms as he kissed her back.

"It's not much of a fantasy really. I just want to be everything for you." She broke away from the kiss to slide her hands between them. Emily stroked his cock with her palm through the fabric of his boxers.

"Fuck, baby, what happened to you?"

"When you were gone I started thinking about you, and then I couldn't stop thinking about you." She slid her hand underneath the band of his boxers, and her hand wrapped around his dick.

Blaine hissed at the intense pleasure. He'd not expected to find this wanton woman. Running his hands up and down her naked body, Blaine was desperate to get inside her.

He whimpered as she climbed off his lap but knelt between his spread thighs.

"What are you doing, baby?" he asked.

"I'm going to give to you what you give me." She pulled his cock out of his briefs. He watched as she licked her lips, stroking the length of his cock. Her hand felt so damn good around his cock.

****

When Blaine had left to go help Whizz with whatever he needed to have done Emily had found herself waiting around bored. There wasn't much of her and Darcy's belongings to move. With the extra peaceful time she picked up one of the sex books her mother loved to give her. What Emily hadn't been expecting was the very explicitly told sex scene of the woman in control of the man's pleasure.

She hadn't been able to stop reading the scene, getting turned on as it described her swallowing the abundance of cum the male hero released. When they were younger she'd tried to suck Blaine's cock, but they'd not gotten to properly enjoy it. He'd gone down on her, and she wanted to give him the same kind of pleasure.

Emily stroked his shaft, watching his reactions. He looked in heaven and hell.

Moving forward, she licked the tip that leaked his pre-cum out of the tiny slit. She closed her eyes, tasting his musk. The taste didn't repulse her, and she continued to lick away his pre-cum, basking in the taste of his cock. Blaine reached out to stroke her hair.

Pulling away, she removed the band she'd put in to have her hair in a ponytail. She fingered out the length before taking hold of his cock once again.

"I love your hair." Blaine began to run his fingers through the length. He released a groan as she sucked the mushroom tip into her mouth. "I love your mouth as well."

She smiled but didn't say anything. Emily loved the taste of him. His pre-cum didn't stop coming even as she licked the tip. She swallowed down his cum, moaning as she took more of him into her mouth.

Blaine wrapped her hair around his fist and started to take control of the depth at which she took him.

His hand went to the base so she had to stop going down. "I don't want you to choke on my cock."

Humming that she understood, Emily cupped his balls as she worked his dick into her mouth. He pumped his length inside her, jerking his hips up. She didn't choke on his length as he stopped her from taking too much of him.

"Your mouth feels so fucking good, Emily. So good."

With his reaction to Nicole, Emily believed his words. They were no longer empty promises but real ones. Tate had told her he'd changed. Everyone, including her parents, had told her he was a changed man. She was the only person who'd not believed him.

Her doubts were not unfounded, but he'd smashed the last of them minutes earlier with their fake neighbor. She still couldn't believe she'd fallen into changing a light bulb and then she'd let the woman stay in case Blaine had come back. There was only one word for her, stupid.

Pushing all the negative thoughts aside, she focused on her man. Blaine was more important than anyone else in that moment.

Taking him as far as he'd let her, she set up a steady rhythm that had him tightening his hand in her hair. Emily murmured her approval as heat spilled between the lips of her sex. The grip he had in her hair turned her on. She liked the edge of pain, but what she liked more was how close to the edge she was making him.

His cock jerked in her mouth, pulsing as he got closer and closer to orgasm.

"Fuck, baby, I'm going to come."

She kept taking him into her mouth. Emily didn't want to stop. This was what she wanted to give him. To show Blaine she was trying to be everything he needed. She had held back for so long that she'd forgotten what it was really like to be a woman with needs.

"Em, baby, if you don't want a mouthful of cum you're going to have to stop."

Emily didn't stop. She kept sucking him into her mouth.

Blaine yelled a curse as his cock jerked filling her mouth with his cum. There was no time to hesitate or panic. Emily swallowed him down, moaning at the taste of him filling her.

"Fuck, baby, fuck," he said, grunting.

She glanced up at him to see his head thrown back in rapt pleasure.

When she'd swallowed the last of his seed, she rested her head against his inner thigh. "Merry Christmas, Blaine."

He started to laugh. Emily didn't have to wait long as he hauled her up his body and rested her against the sofa. "My turn."

She was about to protest when in one quick move he had her panties off her body. Emily cried out the instant he sucked her clit into his mouth.

"You're already wet, baby. You want my mouth or my dick?"

"Both," she said, crying out at the spark of pleasure he created with his mouth.

Gripping his hair, she thrust up to meet his mouth, loving the sounds he made as he fucked her with his tongue before circling her clit.

Within minutes of his touch she was coming apart, knowing she'd made the right decision. It was time to bask in having her Blaine back.

****

Stink looked toward the bar where Sandy was

filling up the drinks. She was laughing and talking with Eva, Baker, and Angel. All the kids were in the center watching cartoons on the large television all the men had put their money together to get. Glancing around the room he saw the men didn't have a problem with all the kids gathered around or even the fact there were cartoons on the screen and not the game. This was what he loved about the club—they were all a family. They all banded together, relied on each other to take care of one another.

"Is it true what they say about you?" Adam asked, coming to sit beside him.

"What's that?"

"You can't smell."

Sandy's laughter caught his attention once again. She'd dyed her hair blonde in the last couple of weeks. He didn't mind what she did to her hair. He'd fallen in love with the woman years ago. Stink had never acted on his feelings, not wanting to put too much pressure on Sandy. She was a skittish woman and had once been a club whore. He knew she'd fucked Tiny at one time as well. Stink didn't care what she had done in her past. Since she'd been staying with him, she'd not been with anyone else. He'd not asked for anything other than her company, not even a kiss.

He doubted she knew how he truly felt for her.

"She taken as well?" Adam asked, nodding toward Sandy.

"You touch her and I'll shoot your dick off."

"What is with everyone threatening bodily harm?" Adam shook his head.

"You keep annoying the brothers you'll be kicked out of the club. Don't touch their women. Don't even pretend to have an interest. You'll lose all votes if you try. We don't go for that shit." He recalled the tension when Zero had thought he was in love with Sophia. Stink didn't want to live through anything like that. Prue had put Zero to rights, but it had been touch and go for a long time.

Sandy left the bar heading back to the kitchen. Angel spent a great deal of time in the kitchen, so Lash had put some mistletoe above the door. Stink had watched the other brother waiting to give Angel a kiss each time she entered.

Getting to his feet, he stood in the doorway watching as Sandy bent over to look into the oven. She rarely cooked, but when she did it was always delicious.

He stared at her beautiful round ass on display. Sandy wasn't a slender woman. In recent years her curves had begun to thicken and get rounder. Stink imagined it was also down to not being on her feet every day. She'd stopped working at the hospital as a doctor. Sandy only worked when she felt like it. The hospital kept trying to lure her back, but she refused.

Her loyalty was to the club, nowhere else.

She stood, putting trays of biscuits on a cooling rack. After several minutes passed, she turned around and let out a little scream.

"Shit, Stink, you scared me." She pressed a hand to her heart.

"I didn't mean to."

"I know that." She started to laugh. "I know you wouldn't try to frighten me."

Sandy walked toward him. Her body drew his gaze like a flame did a moth. She was such a beautiful woman. He loved being around her, but he also knew if he didn't make a move on her soon, she'd be picked up by someone else. Stink didn't want to live with that. His apartment wouldn't ever be the same again without her. He needed her in his life more than he needed anything else.

"What's going on? You look worried." She reached out to touch his hand.

Glancing up, Stink smiled. "Mistletoe."

"He really did do it. I heard Lash saying he was going to find an excuse for Angel to kiss him every time she left the kitchen. I even heard him making a deal with Anthony to get him to call her out." Sandy started laughing.

Stink reached out, wrapping a hand around her waist, and pulling her close.

"Stink, what are you doing?"

The smile left her face. He needed to do this for the both of them.

"I'm taking my kiss."

"Don't do this," she said.

He didn't listen. Sinking a hand into her hair, he held her in place as he took the kiss he'd been desperate for from the moment he first saw her years ago. Stink didn't want to pressure her or risk losing her, but he couldn't go on anymore. Sandy was determined to keep him at arms' length. He loved her and would do anything for her, even risk everything to take this next step.

Her hands went from pushing him away to gripping his shoulders. Encouraged, he slid his tongue across her lip waiting for her to open up to his tongue. After seconds passed, she moaned, opening her lips.

Stink had his first taste of her, and he was greedy as he wanted more. She stroked the back of his neck while he tugged on her hair. He broke away from the kiss to suck at the pulse beside her neck. Stink nibbled on her earlobe until he stopped to whisper to her. "Now you know what I want. I'm not expecting you to fuck me for a chance to stay with me. I want you, Sandy. I've wanted you for a long time. I'll wait for when you're ready, but I'm not going to pretend I don't want you anymore."

With those words finally out in the open, he pulled back to look into her eyes. He gave her a one final kiss, turned, and walked away.

Chapter Nine

Freezing his balls off, Blaine stood out in the cold as the kids made their snowman. It was so fucking cold but it was the weekend, and he'd drawn the short straw to watch over the kids. Baker was inside preparing for the coming Christmas Eve feast, Whizz was organizing the last of the wedding, and the women were gathering the final presents. It was a week until the big Christmas day.

Darcy was now off school for good. His little girl looked so happy nowadays. She was glowing in ways that filled him with pride. Emily was also happier. They couldn't have sex as she'd started her monthly cycle. Last night they'd lain in bed while he rubbed at her stomach to ease out the knots. She'd snuggled up against him to work his magic with his touch. Blaine couldn't complain about life. They were closer than they'd ever been before. He for one loved being with her and the club as their life was better. Blaine had also been back to the apartment to make sure Nicole knew she wasn't to go anywhere near his woman. He wasn't interested in the bitch's excuses. The only woman in his life was Emily. Nicole agreed to stay away. From what his brothers told him, Nicole had been trying to get in with the club for some time. No one wanted anything to do with her. She had a long history of not being safe with her body.

Nicole was now out of the picture for good.

"I'm coming," Tate said.

He glanced toward the back of the clubhouse to see Tate waddling like a penguin toward him. Chuckling, he walked toward her and helped her over the snow. If she took a tumble it would be dangerous for her. Murphy had warned them all about this late stage of pregnancy. She still had a couple of months left, but Tate was huge.

He wondered if she was expecting twins. No one had said she was. If one of the kids was hiding behind the other there was a chance it was missed.

"What are you doing out here?"

"Getting exercise and getting away from Murphy. He won't let me help the others work. It's boring, and you're out here on your own."

"Emily's wrapping the last of the presents." She'd offered to go out, but he was useless at wrapping gifts.

"I know. Kelsey's helping as she had several gifts herself to wrap." Killer and Kelsey had a son, Markus. All of the kids were going to get spoiled, Blaine was sure. Darcy was going to be spoilt as well. "Daddy also asked for some help."

Blaine laughed. He wasn't the only man that was useless at wrapping.

Tate rubbed her hands together as they stood beside each other watching the kids. "It really is awesome we're all here."

His laughter died. It had taken them all a long time to get here, and he said as much.

"I sometimes wonder what it would be like if Mikey was here."

Mikey was one of the original members who'd gotten killed a few years ago. Blaine still went to the cemetery where their fallen was resting.

"What do you mean?"

Tate looked at him. "I'm not stupid. I've heard the talk about my uncle. You all think he's been given too much opportunity to have his say about the club."

"I'm not going to get into that." Blaine wasn't comfortable talking about it. The other brothers did believe it was Alex's influence that had ruined their friendship with the Chaos Bleeds MC.

"I'm not here to pick your brain. Murphy's given me a warning and so has my father. I'm not a club member. I'm a club member's old lady. It used to bother me, but it doesn't anymore. I've seen what it takes to be a member. There's so much stress just being an old lady." Blaine stayed quiet while she talked. "I hear you're going to ask Emily to marry you."

He glanced back toward the clubhouse. Tate could be a bitch at times, and he wouldn't put it past her to go and tell Emily what he wanted to do.

"I've not told her," said Tate. "This life is not for everyone. I remember when The Darkness was a threat. No one had heard from Murphy. I was so scared, and then he arrived home, scarred but he was alive. During that time I thought I'd die before I got a chance to see him again." Tears filled her eyes, and she stopped to take several deep breaths. "Emily's a good woman, and you're a good man. I'm trying to offer you my congratulations."

"While you're also warning me it's not going to be an easy life."

Tate nodded. "I love Murphy. I've always loved him. If there's any doubt in your mind about both of your feelings, then I'd wait. With The Skulls you're either all in or you're out. There's no double loyalty or in between. It's good that Butch is leaving for Vegas."

He'd already talked to Emily about the loyalty of the club. She swore she'd be loyal to him before she was loyal to anyone else. The club would come first to protect Blaine. He couldn't ask for anything more from her.

The sound of the door opening had them both turning toward the sound. Murphy, Killer, and Whizz were making their way out of the door.

"Here comes trouble."

All three men had been at The Lions, another MC

they'd had to take out over the years. Whizz and Killer had been part of the club and hated it. Murphy had vouched for them as he'd only gone to The Lions as a spy in an attempt to find their weakness.

So much had happened in the years he'd been with The Skulls. Blaine wouldn't change a thing. He loved the club, and now he had his woman as well.

"What's going on?" Tate asked.

"Besides the fact you're out here when I told you to rest your fucking ass?" Murphy said, glaring at his woman. Murphy wrapped his arm around Tate. "It's dangerous out here, not to mention cold."

"I was going crazy in there. No one will let me do anything."

"That's because I've told them to let you rest. You're supposed to be resting."

"I'm watching Simon."

"Blaine's out here."

"You're not going to send me in like a kid. I want some fresh air, and you're here now." Tate snuggled up against Murphy.

Blaine laughed as Murphy crumbled, holding her tighter.

"Is everything ready?" Blaine asked, turning his attention to Whizz.

"We're all set. I've got everything. I just need to wait for the day."

"How did it go at the adoption agency?" Killer asked, taking out a cigarette.

"Good and bad. Being with The Skulls is a mark against us and also Lacey's very hazy past doesn't help. The Savage Brothers are known by the cops, or at least some members were growing up, but the problem with Lacey is her attempted suicide when she was younger."

"Surely they can't do shit like that?" Killer asked.

"All the shit she'd been through."

Whizz shrugged. "I'm not giving up. I've got to show a settled environment, and Lacey needs to show a settled living. This gym would help our cause a lot more."

"Why would it?" Blaine asked, interested to know what was going on in his brother's life.

"It's a stable working environment. I've already talked to Tiny, and he's agreed to have Lacey on the books with a decent living." Whizz ran fingers through his hair. "The woman I spoke to knew Mikey. She couldn't guarantee we'd be successful, but she was going to help us to get the chance to adopt. Providing we meet all the requirements, we'll get a kid."

"It's fucking shit if you ask me," Murphy said. "There's so many kids out there who'd be better off being adopted than shifted from place to place. You and Lacey should get kids."

"Look, it sucks, but I get it. I understand why it's hard to get a kid. I just don't want Lacey to feel like she failed. I'm doing this without her knowing. I want to give her this gift. Those bastards took it away, and I'm going to give it to her."

Blaine nodded. Whizz and Lacey deserved some happiness of their own.

"You'll get it, Whizz. Either the old fashioned way by following their rules or just find a weakness and threaten them," Blaine said.

"I'd rather not go that route."

"You know you could put an ad in the paper," Tate said. They all turned to look at her. "What? Ask for a chance to adopt. If a woman doesn't want the kid she's carrying but she doesn't want to abort it, you pay her to allow you to adopt. It's another way of doing it."

Whizz nodded. "You know what, I'll look into

that."

Tate smiled. "See," she said, nudging Murphy in the side. "If you'd made me go inside Whizz wouldn't have heard my idea."

Murphy laughed. "Okay, I was wrong."

"You give in way too easily," Whizz said.

"Fire in the hole," Darcy said.

Blaine gasped as a white snowball landed right in his face. The cold of the ice froze him to the spot.

"You little shits," Murphy said, shouting as more snowballs crashed their way.

Out of the corner of Blaine's eye, he saw the club start to file out. All of them were wrapped in jackets and gloves.

"Snowball fight," Darcy said, shouting for them all to hear.

Blaine noticed his daughter had pulled all the kids behind the climbing frame where they were protected.

Emily walked up beside him. "She got you good." She batted away the snow.

"Darcy's a damn good shot."

"That she is," Emily said, giggling.

****

Emily thought Blaine looked adorable covered in snow. Their daughter had got him good in the face.

Tiny and Eva were throwing snowballs at each other. There was no order, and Emily quickly bent down and started running away from Blaine. The snowball fight was in full swing, but there were no teams. This was a free for all. She threw her snowball, and hers got Blaine in the chest.

Around them the club were laughing, crying out, and having fun. Lash charged at Angel as she threw a snowball that hit him in the nuts. Angel started to dash away, but Lash caught her around the waist, swinging her up in his arms.

Anthony, Tabitha, and Miles were working together as a team to fire as many balls as possible. It looked like Anthony was the best of the three throwers as Miles and Tabitha were molding the snow into balls then handing them to Anthony who threw them out. They were all the next generation of The Skulls. Beside the group of three stood Simon and Rachel who were also there, and behind all of them was Darcy and Michael, Cheryl's son. Michael and Darcy were the oldest, and both were working together to fire snowballs.

With her attention on the kids she'd not heard or seen Blaine sneak up at her until he'd pulled her jacket far enough to stuff snow down. She screamed, rounding on him, intending pain. Blaine kicked out her feet, taking her down to the floor.

"Get off me. Fuck it's freezing."

Blaine chuckled. "That will teach you to take me on, baby."

She looked up into his eyes, and she knew without a doubt she was in love with him. Blaine was her world and would always be her world.

"I love you," she said, cupping his cheek.

The smile vanished from his face as he stared down at her. "Do you mean that?"

She nibbled on her lip. "Yes, I mean that. I've always been in love with you, Blaine. I never stopped."

He pulled off his glove to cup her cheek. "You know how I feel about you."

Emily leaned up, pressing a kiss to his lips. It was a mistake to do as they'd put themselves in the line of sight of their kids, The Skulls the next generation.

They got a snowball in the face.

Pulling away, Blaine got to his feet, jerking her up with him. They rounded the wall for cover. She wiped the snow off her face.

"You do realize our daughter just interrupted our moment."

"We should tell Santa. No more presents for her," Emily said.

She was so happy. It had been years since she'd felt like this. In that moment she understood what her mother was trying to do. Without giving herself to Blaine or trusting him, she'd not really been living, only existing. Shirley had known she wasn't truly living or enjoying life. Emily hadn't realized she'd been getting by from day to day. The last few weeks with Blaine had been joyous to her.

They were finally together, and she'd never been happier. She would call her mother to thank her when they were done punishing their daughter.

Out of the corner of eye she saw Murphy was walking Tate inside.

"She's heavily pregnant and would probably do herself an injury?" Blaine said.

"Come on out, Mom," Darcy said.

"It's a trick," Emily said. "She's never so nice."

Blaine laughed.

Reaching forward, Emily grabbed a handful of snow.

"She got this from you, didn't she?" Blaine asked.

"What do you mean?" Emily glanced behind her to see Blaine laughing.

"You've always had a mean throw. I'd forgotten about it."

Emily paused as she remembered their first Christmas together when she was seventeen. He had taken her to the café in town where they'd shared a muffin and a coffee. On the way home they'd gone through the church gates, and on the way out, she'd bent down to gather up some snow.

"If you hit me in the chest, I'll give you a kiss."

She'd pretended not to know what she was doing and had thrown the snowball at him.

"Okay, do it twice. Beginners' luck."

Shooting a second time she'd got him in the chest. The kiss afterward had been amazing. Her first ever kiss by a boy.

"I've always been good at throwing."

"Yeah, Shirley told me why."

Her father had put up a basketball hoop in the back garden. Emily had used it more than he did. She had practiced her aim and could get every single ball within the hoop.

"Come on, we can get our daughter."

Standing tall, Emily threw the ball getting Darcy in the chest. Within the hour they were all cold but laughing. She walked the kids back into the clubhouse. Darcy wouldn't shut up and kept talking.

"It was totally funny, Mom. I mean, seriously, you and Dad were right there and it was totally too hard to resist. I thought it was funny. Grandma and Granddad said I'd be a good shot just like you if I practiced all the time. I practice all the time. Do you think I'm a good shot? That was totally awesome. I love it here. Are we staying here? Are we going to visit here often? Michael's so funny, and he's got like two dads."

Emily laughed while Blaine looked like he was struggling to keep up.

She talked Darcy into the bath while Blaine took the first shower. When Darcy was dressed in some pajamas Blaine came through dressed in some clean, dry clothes.

"Will you keep an eye on her while I go and get

freshened up?"

"Go."

Leaving them together, she made her way toward their bathroom. She pulled out her cell phone and dialed her mother's number.

"Hey, honey, we're having an awesome time here at the cruise," Shirley said.

"Hey, Mom." Emily took a seat on the toilet.

"What's going on? Are you having fun? Does your father need to come back and kick his ass?"

Emily chuckled. "No, you don't need to come and kick Blaine's ass. It's fine. No, it's perfect. It's exactly how I imagined it."

Shirley was silent on the line. Emily heard noise across the line and shuffling as if her mother was moving.

"Mom?"

"I've come back to the room, honey. You don't sound happy."

"I'm happy. I'm really happy. I told Blaine I loved him."

"That's good, Emily. You've always been in love with him."

Emily let out a breath. "I don't know what's going on with me right now."

"I'll give you a clue. It's called forgiveness. It's about time. You've been putting that boy through the wringer the last few years. I wouldn't mind, but I knew you weren't happy."

"I'm happy now, Mom."

"You see why you should always listen to your parents?"

She laughed. "I love you, Mom."

"I love you too, darling. Your father and I couldn't have been prouder of you. We both know the last few years haven't been easy for you."

"It was my fault."

"Darcy is an angel, and you've been blessed with having a man who knows he's got the best. Blaine's not going to let you down, and if he thinks he can your father's got a gun to shoot him. I've got to get back before you father misses me."

"Merry Christmas, Mom."

"Merry Christmas, darling. We'll always be here for you."

Emily disconnected the call, glancing up toward the light as tears filled her eyes. Her mother had a way of putting life into perspective.

She had a quick shower, changing into a skirt and a white shirt. Making her way downstairs she found Blaine and Darcy were playing a board game. She entered the kitchen to find the women and Baker hard at work. Angel stood in front of Baker as he held a pastry toward her.

Angel moaned. "That's delicious."

This was home. Being around these women and being with Blaine was what made this home to her.

****

"Rose, are you sure about this?" Tiny asked, lifting up the file she'd had the lawyer write up. It was her divorce papers.

"I'm sure. It's time I take matters into my own hands."

"It's Christmas and you're going for a divorce."

Sitting in the chair inside Tiny's office, Rose's heart started to split in two. She'd never been good at confrontation, and in the last few weeks her life had been nothing but confrontation.

"I'm not trying to make the festive season miserable." She stopped to lick her lips. Baker had encouraged her to come back to the clubhouse. The Skulls hadn't turned their backs on her, and neither had Hardy. She'd been the one to turn her back on Hardy. "This is what I need to do."

Tiny got up from his seat to round the desk and sit down. Her was a large man and had aged gracefully. She imagined that had to do with Eva. No one could hate Eva, as she was loved by the whole of the club.

"I've got Ned Walker coming in for Christmas. The clubhouse is made up to the nines. All the kids are present, Alex is pissing me off being evasive, and you've thrown a divorce into the mix." Tiny leaned back to put the file onto his desk. "I can't get him to sign it."

"Hardy won't sign it until he's ready. I've already made arrangements. In time he'll see that it's useless in trying to keep me."

Tiny frowned. "What are you going to do, Rose?"

"I'm going to prove to my husband that I'm moving on. It's time he does as well."

"What does that mean?"

"I'm going on a date." Rose wanted a fresh start, a clean one away from Hardy. She loved the club, but after this Christmas she was going to take a step away from it. In the weeks she'd been alone she'd started applying for work. She was determined to land on her own two feet.

"Who with?"

"No one you know." Rose got to her feet. She held her hand out to Tiny. "I want to thank you for everything you've done for me."

"There's no way I can change this?" he asked.

Rose grew sad. "The only way you can change that is if you can change Hardy, and that's never going to happen."

She made her way toward the door.

"I'm sorry," he said.

Glancing back at him she saw a deep sadness in Tiny. "Why? This is not your fault."

"If I'd been a better leader, a better president, Hardy wouldn't have done this to you. I'd have known what was going on before it was too late."

Rose released a sigh. "You're not the one in control of Hardy's dick. He knew what he was doing, and all I did was make it easy for him. This is not on us, Tiny. This is Hardy."

She opened the door allowing it to close behind her. Hardy stood there, waiting.

"Are you ever going to leave me alone?"

"Are you going to stop trying to divorce me?" he asked.

The spicy scent of baking filled every one of her senses. She loved Christmas and had planned for it for years where she'd have children. The children hadn't happened, and neither had anything else. Her life had been put on hold for this man.

"No, I'm not going to try to stop divorcing you. You're going to realize you can't have everything you want."

"I realized I couldn't have everything I want when you wouldn't get pregnant."

The pain was instant. Instead of hitting out at home, Rose became more determined. "Well, divorce me and you'll find another whore to impregnate." She stormed away, going toward the kitchen where her friends were. Hardy wasn't going to take away her friends. She'd given up on him, not their friends.

****

"That was fucking cold," Tiny said, coming out of his office.

Hardy didn't need a lecture. He already knew

he'd fucked up the moment he said the words.

"I got angry."

"She's right. You're a selfish bastard, and she's put up with it for years. We've fed your need." Tiny slammed the file against his chest. "You can handle this. As far as I'm concerned, she deserves to be away from you."

The disgust on Tiny's face hurt, but Hardy had already known he'd fucked up. He'd wanted to hurt Rose like her need to be away from him was hurting him.

He needed to get his shit together and make a change before he completely lost the woman he loved.

SAM CRESCENT

Chapter Ten

Blaine caressed his hands down Emily's naked back. Christmas was days away, and she'd finally admitted her feelings toward him. He couldn't stop smiling as he remembered her telling him she loved him. Darcy was in bed after an afternoon of making snowmen and snowball fighting. It had been fun watching the kids. Millie had also turned up with another bag of toys for them to wrap.

He'd invited Millie to his upcoming wedding as well. She asked if Emily knew about the wedding. When he told her not, he saw the joy fill Millie's eyes. He could tell the little toyshop owner was charmed by his act of romance.

If it hadn't been for Whizz he wouldn't have been able to organize anything.

"You're just going to tease me?" she asked.

"I'm playing with my favorite toy."

"I'm a toy now?" She glanced behind her to smile.

"You're my toy. I don't like sharing my toy."

He pushed the blanket off her back and climbed over to straddle her legs. Blaine began to work out her muscles, massaging her back. She moaned and spread her arms out wide. "You know exactly what to do to have me melting for you, don't you?"

"You're responsive to my touch."

Working out the knots in her back, he slid his other hand down to go between the cheeks of her ass. He worked down, pressing a finger inside her creamy cunt. Her monthly cycle had ended last night, and he'd taken full advantage, filling her up with his cum. He knew it was useless, but he hoped he'd be able to convince her to

139

have more children with him. Blaine wanted a house full of kids to look forward to. He imagined Shirley and Lenard would love to have more grandchildren.

The finger that he'd put inside her, he moved up to caress her swollen clit.

She whimpered, lifting her ass up a little.

"Get on your knees."

Emily moved to her knees, groaning he filled her with two fingers.

"I want you to reach into the drawer by my side. Get me the lube, baby."

Blaine let her go and spread the cheeks of her ass wide to see the puckered hole of her anus and the sweet entrance to her cunt. He saw his cum still leaked out of her pussy.

They very sight had his cock straining up as if to get closer to her.

She handed him the lubrication he'd bought just for this moment. Emily had a bit of a dark side to her. Blaine had found her dirty books and knew she wasn't as innocent as she made out. There hadn't been any other man between her thighs, but those books she read sure liked to go into detail. He was more than happy to provide his woman with the means of living out those fantasies as there were several of his own he'd like to explore.

With the lubrication close to him, he began to tease her pussy once again. He wanted her as wet as possible before he tried to fuck her ass. Blaine worked three fingers inside her, and with his other hand, he pinched her clit.

Emily writhed on the bed pushing back against him to make him go deeper.

"Please, Blaine, I need your cock."

Slapping her ass, he leaned down and pressed a

kiss to her sting. "Be patient. You'll have my cock when I'm ready to give it to you."

She whimpered but stayed still as he went back to playing with her cunt and clit.

He tapped her clit as her pussy contracted around his fingers. She was so close to orgasm. Blaine pulled away, not wanting to make it too easy for her. Emily growled in frustration but didn't voice her thoughts. It was probably a good thing she didn't as he'd spank her ass until she was red.

Picking up the lube, he flipped the cap off and pressed a good amount of the clear gel onto his fingers. He put the tube down, then worked his slick fingers over her asshole. She tensed up, but seconds later she eased down giving him time to play with her pretty ass.

"That's it, baby, you know you're going to like my cock inside you." He stroked her cheek while he worked one finger past the tight ring of muscles. Blaine took his time, waiting for her to push back to him. He wasn't in a rush to get it over with. "Can you take a second finger?"

She didn't respond as he eased a second wet finger into her ass. When he had both fingers in her tight ass with ease, Blaine pulled out and worked more of the gel over his cock. He got himself nice and covered with plenty of lubrication.

Moving behind her, he aligned the tip with her anus.

"If at any time you're in pain and need me to stop just let me know. I'm not going to hurt you, Emily."

"I will. I trust you."

Pushing the mushroom head of his cock against her ass, he tightened his hand on her hip as he eased the tip into her ass. Emily fought him at first, the tight muscles of her ass keeping him out, but he was determined and she'd not voiced any protest. "Push out."

She did as he asked, and he got the tip of his cock inside her ass. Emily groaned, lifting up from the bed to glance behind her. Her eyes were dilated. The arousal was clear to see as he looked at her.

"You've got the tip of me inside your ass, baby. I'm there." He worked another inch of his cock inside her. Once there was enough of him within her ass, Blaine gripped her hips and slowly, inch by inch glided into her ass. She was incredibly tight, hot, and Blaine made sure to take his time. If he wasn't careful he could seriously hurt her, and that was something he didn't want to do.

"It feels strange," she said. He heard her exhale several times along with sharp inhales.

When the last inch of him was inside her, he paused giving her time to get used to the feel of him. "You've got all of me right now, baby."

"I don't know if I can take much more, Blaine."

"Touch your clit." All the books she read had anal sex in them. He'd taken the time to read the advisories. Blaine had bought her a precious e-reader with a voucher so she had enough to fill the device. When they'd been together while she was still in high school she'd loved to read. A few times they would sit together and she would read to him. He loved listening to her read. He doubted she would want to share the stories she was reading now with him. Blaine didn't mind.

The moment she touched her clit, Blaine cursed. Her ass seemed to get tighter around his cock. Emily's moan was stifled by the pillow underneath her, but he heard it. His woman was as desperate for release as he was. Blaine began to count sheep waiting for the joyous moment when she pushed back against him. Emily wasn't able to wait long for her pleasure. The moment she started to get frustrated she'd try to rush him along.

Blaine wasn't interested in being rushed. He intended to take his sweet time with Emily's ass.

She played with her clit, which only tortured him more.

Gripping her hips, he stared down at where they were joined. Her ass was open around his cock.

He groaned, moving his thumb down to touch where they were joined.

"I wish you could see this. I wish you could see how fucking hot you look with my dick in your ass."

Emily gasped, and he was sure he felt her press back.

Running his thumb around his shaft right where they were connected, he waited for her to push back against him. He didn't know how much longer he could hold onto his sanity.

****

Emily gritted her teeth. She'd come to realize Blaine would wait for her to give the signal of pushing back against him before he'd fuck her. In trying to torture him, she was also torturing herself. It wasn't fair.

Giving in, Emily pushed back against him, trying to intensify the pleasure and to feel him explode inside her.

"You little vixen. You know that I won't do anything until you show me you want it."

He gripped her hips, pressing himself a little deeper inside her. Blaine wasn't a small man. He was large in all the right places, but the way he pressed the last inch inside her was on the verge of pain. She stroked a finger over her clit. It was strange to her to have her ass filled and her pussy empty. Moving down, she slid two fingers inside her, groaning as she pressed against the thin wall that separated her from Blaine's cock.

"I feel your fingers rubbing against me, Emily.

Do you like that?"

"Yes."

"I'll get a dildo so you know what it's like to be fucked in the cunt and ass. You'll not be getting two men near you. I don't share. Those kinds of fantasies are going to stay in those books you read."

She gasped, shocked that he knew the kind of books she read in her free time.

"You can't keep anything away from me." He leaned over her back until his breath brushed her ear. "Knowing you love those kinds of books turns me on, Emily. We can practice some of those moves if you'd like." He licked the pulse at her neck, and Emily shook at the pleasure.

Moving her fingers back to her clit she couldn't contain her excitement anymore. She needed to come.

Blaine began to work his cock in and out of her ass. The lube made it easy for him to work his cock. She pushed back against him trying to make him speed up, but his grip on her hips stopped her from taking over.

"You're going to hurt yourself, Emily."

"Please, I need you, Blaine."

"Stop messing around and touch that clit."

She fingered her clit, pulling back the hood and stroking around the nub.

"I'm not going to move until you come, and then I'm going to fuck your ass. You're going to take all of my cum, Emily, like you do when you suck my dick. Watching you swallow my load is the hottest thing I've ever seen."

His words drove her toward another orgasm. Crying out, she shuddered as she kept up the strokes on her clit.

"That's it, baby, give it all to me. Let me hear you scream my name."

SAM CRESCENT

Emily screamed his name as her orgasm continued. Only when she couldn't stand any more pleasure did she stop touching herself. Blaine, true to his word, fucked her ass, showing her it was just as good in real life as it sounded in the books.

He didn't hold anything back, giving her a hard fucking. She pushed back, crying out as with one final thrust he erupted inside her.

When it was over, he remained inside her ass, and they collapsed on the bed together.

"Okay, now that has to be one of the best things that I've ever experienced," she said, pushing hair out of her face.

Blaine chuckled, banding an arm around her waist.

"I want to ask you a question, Emily."

She twisted her head to look at him. "What is it?"

"Will you stop taking your pill?"

Emily stared at him, wondering what he was trying to say. She knew what he was saying, but at the same time she didn't know.

"I love you, Emily. I'm not going to back out of this. We're in this for the long haul. I want more children. I want to be there in ways I wasn't with for Darcy. Your mother told me about the birth, how hard it was for you and how you wished I was there."

Throughout the whole of the labor she'd kept glancing at the door hoping that Blaine would come through the door and prove to her she'd been wrong. When it came to Blaine, she'd always wanted to be wrong.

You've been wrong about him now.

"You do know what you're asking?"

"Yes. I'm asking for you to trust me. I want to have a family with you. We talked about it all the time."

Emily bit her lip unsure what to say to him.

Trust him.

"I'll stop taking the pill." She'd not taken it that night.

"Thank you." He pressed a kiss to her lips. The moment his lips were on hers, she lost all sense. She loved being a mother, and Darcy always asked for a brother or sister.

"Come on. It's time I washed you."

Emily winced as he eased out of her ass. She now understood why Blaine had kept a firm grip on her hips. If he hadn't she would have been in a lot more pain.

He picked her up, and she held onto him. There was no point arguing with Blaine. He'd do what he wanted anyway. When they were in the bathroom, he put her on the floor while he ran the bath that was along the other wall. She'd not been in the bath tub, preferring to take long showers.

Blaine eased her into the warm water, sitting behind her as they both sank down to the water. She moaned, loving the feel of the warm water around her. Emily didn't say anything to Blaine, but it also eased out the pain that was in her ass.

She doubted she'd be having anal sex any time again soon, but she did love it. Blaine stroked his fingers over her arms and locked their fingers together. She saw her name was printed on the inside of his arm. Turning his arm over, she looked at the writing, touched by the marking he held of her on his body. Blaine had a lot of ink over his body, and she couldn't believe she'd never seen her name on his arm before. She traced the name across his arm. Turning to his other hand she saw Darcy's name scribbled across his inner arm, but it wasn't as big.

"I'm going to put all of their names on my arm."

"Whose names?"

"Our kids."

He kissed her temple, and Emily smiled, touched by his kindness.

"I love you, Blaine."

"And I love you, baby. I'm never going to forget what you mean to me."

Chapter Eleven

The big day had finally arrived. Blaine saw the kids loved the special pancakes Angel was making with the chocolate chips. He saw Whizz calling the priest to come and get them both married. In his pocket he held the rings that would bind Emily to him for good. He let out a breath as he took in every single one of The Skulls. This was his club and his very reason for being given a second chance.

"Are you nervous?" Lash asked, coming to sit beside him.

"A little. Who wouldn't be?"

"I wouldn't be, but then I know Angel would never leave me hanging. Are you sure about Emily?"

"I'm sure. She's the love of my life."

Lash nodded in agreement. "Women, we're lost without them and yet terrified of losing them all the time when they're around."

Blaine frowned. "You'll never lose Angel. She's in love with you."

"I know, but I can't always protect her. There's not a lot I can do to change the shit that's happening. Tiny wants me to take over, and *that* I'm terrified will cost me Angel. One wrong decision and she's dead."

Blaine understood Lash's fears, but they were unfounded. Lash would do anything to protect his woman and protect the club.

There was the ringing on the club door, and Blaine frowned. "Who the fuck would be ringing the bell?"

"It'll be Millie," Eva said, shouting across the loud noise of the television.

Baker opened the door, and there stood Millie,

shaking as she smiled. "Hey, Blaine invited me."

"I better go," Blaine said.

"Come in." Baker stepped aside but not far enough to give Millie room. The clueless woman had to brush past Baker to get inside.

"You made it."

Millie was a hugger, and she wrapped her arms around him quickly. "I wouldn't miss it. Does she know yet?"

"No, not yet. Do you think you could keep it quiet a little longer?" he asked.

"Your secret is safe with me. I promise." Her smile was pure beauty. Blaine loved his woman and wouldn't dream of straying from her, but he saw the kindness in the woman before him, and the raw beauty that many passed over nowadays. Not only was she kind but she was clueless to her beauty and to the biker currently stalking her. The look in Baker's eyes left Blaine in no doubt that he wanted a piece of Millie.

Emily walked downstairs with Darcy. The moment both of his girls spotted Millie, they called her name and charged into the room.

Millie went down on one knee fisting bumping with Darcy, who giggled back at her.

"You're so cool," Darcy said.

"I wonder how long that'll last." Millie got to her feet and embraced Emily. "It's good to see you."

"Everything is cool to her."

He watched all the women wondering what was going on in Baker's head when he looked at Millie. The guy hadn't turned away. His gaze was so focused on her.

"What brings you here?"

Everyone froze in the room.

"Christmas cards," Millie said. "I'm such a dork. When I delivered the last of the presents I was supposed to leave a card. I completely forgot." She rummaged in her jacket, opening it up and pulling out pristine cards. "Here." She pushed them toward Emily, tucking some hair behind her ear.

"Would you like to stay for dinner?" Blaine asked, quickly thinking on his feet so Emily wouldn't know what was going on.

"I'd love to." Millie smiled, following behind Emily. "I've got your back."

When they were alone once again, Blaine looked at Baker. "What's going on inside that head of yours?"

"Nothing."

"You've got a thing for Millie?"

"No." Baker shook himself. "Not at all."

Before he could ask anything more, Baker walked away. Whizz came downstairs and moved toward him. "Everything is ready. I'll have her parents on video link in ten minutes."

Blaine nodded. He went back upstairs to go to his drawer where he'd stored the wedding band along with the engagement ring Lenard had given him.

When he got back downstairs he followed Whizz through to a room. Lenard and Shirley smiled back at him from a television screen.

"Okay, that's freaky."

"We can wheel it out when you're ready," Whizz said. "I'll give you some time."

He faced Emily's parents taking a deep breath. "Thank you for being here."

"Are you nervous?"

"No, yes, I'm not nervous about marrying her. I'm nervous about her saying no."

"She won't say no. Emily loves you. Always has and always will," Shirley said. "I couldn't be prouder of you, Blaine. You worked so hard."

"I wouldn't have been able to do it without you. I never thanked you for paying for the rehab I went to—"

"There's no need for you to talk about that, son. We did what we could for the man our daughter loved. Emily's yours now, and we expect you treat her with love and kindness. I don't want to have to listen to her sobbing in the phone."

"I won't let it happen. When Lacey and Whizz have married, I'm going to get down on one knee. I wanted you both to be here and I know Emily would."

"We're awesome parents. Everyone wants us."

He chuckled. "I'll agree with that."

"Go and have some fun with Emily and Darcy. It's Christmas, and it's about fun."

Blaine turned the television off, wishing her parents a good day. He took another deep breath, and pulled the rings out of his pockets.

Please say yes, baby. I promise you I'll be a good husband to you.

He did something he'd not done in a long time. He sent a little prayer above in the hope it would be answered.

****

Emily wiped under her eyes as she watched Lacey and Whizz become man and wife. They were both a beautiful couple, startlingly so. They had both been through so much, and they suited each other. Blaine held her hand, tightening his fingers through hers. Her heart pounded inside her chest, and she giggled as Whizz carried Lacey toward the back of the clubhouse.

Silence fell onto the clubhouse, and some jerking on her hand had her turning toward Blaine. She held her breath as he got down one knee. Out of the corner of her eye she saw a television screen being turned on. Her parents came into view.

"Mom, Dad?"

"Hey, honey."

"What's going on?" She returned her attention to Blaine down on one knee before her. Darcy stood behind her looking so happy that it lifted Emily's spirit.

"Emily, from the first moment I saw you I fell in love with you. I've not stopped loving you or wanting you. I knew all those years ago when you were seventeen that you'd be mine. I waited for you even though you didn't want me to." Her cheeks heated as she had begged him more than once to take her. "I fucked up and I hurt you, but I never stopped loving you." Tears filled her eyes as she saw they had also filled his. "I want you to be my wife, and I promise you with the whole of my heart that I will love, honor, and cherish you. I'll never look at another woman. You're the only one for me."

Her heart pounded inside her chest. "You want to marry me?"

"More than anything."

She didn't know what to say. The tears that filled her eyes spilled down her cheeks.

"Please, baby, don't keep me waiting."

"Em, you're torturing the boy," her father said.

"Yes, I love you, and I'll marry you."

Blaine got to his feet wrapping his arms around her. He lifted her hand up and slid one thing on her finger. "I'm afraid it's not a long engagement."

She saw her grandmother's engagement ring. Smiling, she touched Blaine's cheek. "It's perfect."

He took her arm, and they approached the priest. She saw Blaine give Darcy something. Listening to the priest say the exact same words as he had for Whizz and Lacey, Emily spoke when told to, agreeing to love, honor, and cherish Blaine. He'd thought of everything including a ring for himself. She loved the diamond ring he slid onto her finger.

"I now pronounce you husband and wife."

Blaine grabbed her face and slammed his lips down on hers. She was finally his wife. When they broke away the club was cheering for them. Darcy wrapped her arms around the two.

Blaine reached down, picking their daughter up.

"This is a good way to always remember Christmas Eve." Blaine gripped the back of her neck, not allowing her the chance to escape. She loved the way his fingers teased her pulse at the side of her neck.

Millie rushed toward her, holding her close as she accepted all of their congratulations.

"This is your family now, Emily," Tiny said, pulling her in for a hug. Each one of the brothers offered her their acceptance with a hug.

When it was over she went back to her husband, and Blaine took a kiss from her lips. "I had no idea you were going to propose."

"I've been trying to keep it quiet. I thought Millie would let the cat out of the bag."

Emily burst out laughing. "The cards were something she made up?"

"Pretty much."

She didn't mind. Blaine wrapped his arms around her, and she collapsed against him. The rest of the day passed with keeping the kids entertained. Later in the evening Whizz and Lacey came downstairs to gather for the fair Tiny organized. Millie had helped Baker to deliver his baked goods to the town. They all left the clubhouse together. Wrapped up for the cold weather, Emily held Blaine's hand, and he had Darcy on his shoulders as they walked toward the town. The Christmas lights were all aglow, and the town was humming with activity. She stayed by Blaine's side as they made their way toward the bakery stand. Behind the stall Millie was helping Baker to dish out his baked goods. They looked happy together.

Blaine and Darcy grabbed a cream filled éclair, bringing her one. Together they stood in the town square as the tree was lit up by Tiny. Fort Wills was owned by The Skulls, and no one could take it away from them.

"You're my old lady now," Blaine said, kissing her temple. She gazed up into the face of the love of her life. Emily had no doubt her life with Blaine wouldn't be easy. He was a biker, and The Skulls always found trouble. She'd be loyal to him and would never turn her back on him.

The night wore on, and she accepted the congratulations of the town. When it was getting late and Darcy looked ready to fall asleep where she stood the whole of the club started the trek back, but Emily noticed that they were moving toward the graveyard.

"What's going on?"

"I don't know."

Blaine held Darcy as they followed the club. She saw the graveyard read Mikey and beside him were Gunn and Time.

"We've lost some good men and good women. They're here laying to rest. I appreciate you all following me," Tiny said. "In a few years' time I'll be stepping down, and Lash will be taking my place. I ask for you all to give him the same respect that you've shown me. It's Christmas, a time for remembering. I want you all to remember the ones who have given their lives for the good of the club. Lacey, Emily, your men are with the club. I expect the both of you to have the same loyalty to them."

Emily nodded and saw Lacey was doing the same.

The club came first.

She'd given her loyalty to Blaine, and the only way to keep him alive was to swear her loyalty to the club. Emily didn't have a problem with doing it. She'd do everything to keep her husband alive.

A cool breeze ran through the graveyard making goosebumps erupt along her arms despite the warm clothes she wore.

Her gut tightened as she knew something was coming. Life at The Skulls wouldn't remain peaceful for long, but she pushed all of her fears aside. It was Christmas after all, and no one was going to spoil it.

The End

EVERNIGHT PUBLISHING ®

www.evernightpublishing.com